sweethearts

I. S. Belle

contents

eBook ISBN: 978-0-473-69781-5

IngramSpark Print ISBN: 978-0-473-69780-8

KDP Paperback ISBN: 979-8-870-42106-3

content warnings

You know the drill, folks! Here's where you can back out if the following doesn't sound like your cup of tea:

Possession, choking, homophobia, murder, violence, fire, scars, animal death, references to substance abuse and child abuse.

Eat my dust.
— Frankie Tanner's Yearbook Quote, 2005

chapter one

It was the last day of high school and Frankie Tanner was bleeding.

She stuck her stinging finger into her mouth, annoyed. Her yearbook sat on the cafeteria table in front of her. Class of 2005. Despite everything that had happened, they'd made it to the end of senior year. She'd only gotten her yearbook out to check they'd put her quote in properly. She wouldn't put it past them to add a typo on purpose or even omit it entirely. But when she flipped to her name, getting a papercut in the process, there it was, sitting neatly under her scowling photo.

"Cute," said a voice over her shoulder.

Frankie yelped. "Ivy! Jesus!"

Ivy beamed, flipping her new hair: blonde except for a thick black line sliding down the fringe. Frankie had to stop herself from smiling like an idiot every time she saw it.

Ivy sunk down into the cafeteria seat across from her. "I *was* joking, you know. About remembering to smile—"

"I did smile! The cameraman was being a dick." Frankie frowned, remembering the man's nervous leer. *Think of nice things, like dead footballers*, he'd told her. Big talk, but he'd flinched when she got up.

Frankie—or *Loser Tanner,* as they called her—had always been an outcast. But Homecoming, junior year, made it so much worse.

The official story was that a crazy homeless woman came in and set the place on fire. But everyone in that gym had seen the recently deceased April Tanner, see-through and bleeding in front of her screaming sister. Everybody heard about Marvin Martin's body in the bathrooms, already dead before the flames got to him. Everybody knew Frankie and

3

her best friend Ivy Wexler were the last people to leave the gym, clutching each other like girls with a horrible secret.

People avoided Frankie before. Now they *fled* from her, jerking away from her in the hallways that got emptier and emptier the longer the thornfruit fields stayed barren. Bulldeen High was a ghost town, and Frankie was thankful: if more people were here, there would be more people to gang up on her. Scared classmates she could handle. A rude cameraman was fine. Frankie couldn't deal with a mob.

"We could get KJ to sign it." Ivy reached across the table and turned the yearbook around. She flipped back to the front page, all that unsigned space, blank except for Frankie's blood spot.

Frankie made a face. "Seems pretty pathetic. What, want me to corner him in the frozen food section?" Frankie put on a whiny voice. "*KJ, I know you graduated, but no one at school will sign my yearbook. Help a sister out?*"

All that fuss about getting out of town the second he could, and KJ had stuck around and got a job at the Shop N' Save. Saving up money, he insisted. He would follow them to New York in a few weeks. Only one time had he admitted the reason they all knew: *Somebody's gotta keep you girls out of trouble.* He'd laughed like it was a joke. Like they hadn't gotten someone killed. Frankie didn't feel *terrible* about Marvin's death, obviously. He was a shithead. But she didn't feel good about it, either.

Ivy produced a ballpoint pen from her backpack. "Well, we can't just leave it all empty like that."

The fluorescent cafeteria lights bounced off Ivy's scars. She was wearing short sleeves again, to her parents' dismay. Thanks to Frankie's temporarily undead sister, Ivy's right arm was home to two scooped scars. The skin grafts had helped fill them out, but they were still noticeable divots: one on her shoulder, one on the inside of her elbow.

Ivy slid the yearbook back. "Ta-da!"

Frankie laughed. *Have fun in NYC,* it said. *Love, Ivy.*

4

She'd transformed the bloodstain into a dot over the *i*. Frankie touched it. It smeared.

Ivy swatted her wrist. "Don't ruin my artwork!"

"Have fun in NYC," Frankie read out. "That makes it sound like—"

"Oh no, I'm *coming*." Ivy nudged their shoes together under the table. "How else will I make sure you have fun?"

Frankie itched to touch her hand. They'd hold hands in New York. In public, even. Maybe not at first, but they'd build up to it. For now, Bulldeen was still Bulldeen. There were maybe twenty other people in the cafeteria—and yet. And *yet*. Even with every one of those students determinedly ignoring them, even on the last day of school, even with their glorious escape on the horizon—they couldn't risk it. The closest they could get was this: sitting across from each other, a bloody yearbook between them, their shoes barely touching.

"New York," Frankie said. It meant *soon*.

"New York," Ivy agreed.

The last day of school. Two weeks until graduation. And then the rest of their lives.

Dinner at the Wexlers used to mean boring small talk that turned to boring silence once the talk ran out. Nowadays it meant Ivy and Frankie talking about movies, homework, and Frankie's bakery job while Ivy's parents sat there and made bewildered humming noises. Once in a while they even chimed in.

"Remind me who Hadley is again," asked Ivy's dad, poking at the last of his salad. Dinner went faster when you didn't talk.

"KJ's childhood friend," Ivy said.

"KJ's pen pal," Frankie said over her, and tapped Ivy's wrist in apology. "Sorry, you go."

Ivy tapped Frankie's wrist: *apology accepted*. "Hadley lived here for like a year in grade school, now he's over in

New York. KJ hit him up after he decided to follow us out there."

Ivy's parents hummed in time.

"And he says there are pottery classes?" Ivy's mom asked, dabbing at her mouth with a napkin. The Wexlers were a full-on napkin family, fabric and everything, a fact that always made Frankie feel like she was underdressed.

"There *are*," Ivy said, so excited Frankie had to chew her cheek to stop a wild smile. She hadn't known Ivy was interested in pottery. *I didn't either*, Ivy confessed after KJ told her about it. It made Frankie weirdly emotional to think about everything Ivy would grow into. And Frankie would be right there at her side, watching it happen. They were going to grow up together.

Ivy's mom politely waited until Ivy was done talking about the pottery classes. Then she said, "That's lovely. You should talk to that boy more often."

"We haven't chatted," Ivy said, looking at Frankie for help.

Frankie jumped in. "Hadley just knows us as the girls KJ's moving with. And him and KJ aren't even that close."

Another joint hum from Ivy's parents, their eyes meeting in a way that made Frankie squirm.

"Well—oops, sorry." Ivy's mom set her glass down with a loud thump. "We do hope you find other friends in New York."

"It's great you're so close," Ivy's dad continued, tone measured in a way that meant they'd rehearsed this earlier. "You two have been through a lot together."

"But it's good to have more friends," Ivy's mom added. "You can't just…pour everything into one friend. You two act like you're besotted."

Ivy's dad nodded. "Like young sweethearts."

They chuckled, like they didn't give their daughter and her secret girlfriend twin heart attacks at the kitchen table.

Then Ivy's mom's smile dropped, eyes wide. "Not that—of course we don't think *that*. Anybody who says that is just..."

"Jealous of your friendship," Ivy's dad finished.

Ivy's fingers were white around her fork. Eyes on her chicken.

A drop of sweat slid down Frankie's back, her armpits pricking with damp. "Ha ha," she said, her smile wooden. "Yeah." She crammed a mouthful of salad into her mouth. Too much. Celery stabbed her throat as she swallowed, eyes watering.

"Hey," she rasped. "This was great, but I think I'm gonna—"

Ivy's chair screeched back. "Great idea. Mom, Dad, thanks for dinner."

Her parents called something after them as they ran down the hall. Frankie didn't hear it, blood thumping too loud in her ears.

"I don't think they suspect," Frankie mumbled into Ivy's hair. They were on her bed, curled around each other like much younger kids.

Ivy huffed a laugh. It hit Frankie's collarbone, warm and familiar.

"Seriously," Frankie said. "We could make out in front of them and they'd be like *ahhh, what good bosom buds.*"

"Let's not try that." Ivy sniffed, pulling back. Her eyes were red-rimmed. Frankie thumbed the corners of her lashes, trying to imagine them older and fearless underneath towering skyscrapers. Holding hands in public. Taking pottery classes. Living a life far away from this rotting little town where people crossed the street to avoid them.

Ivy sniffed again. "No, you're right. We could get *married* in front of them and they wouldn't suspect. Not that we can get married, but..."

"Yeah." Frankie stroked the black streak in Ivy's hair. She'd been the one to smear the dye in, Ivy's head dripping over the bathroom sink as Frankie read out the instructions. They'd talked about going to a hairdresser, somewhere out of town so no one gave them wary looks or pointedly ignored them—but Ivy insisted. *I want it to be you.*

Ivy leaned up and nudged their foreheads together. "I'd marry you if I could."

Frankie swallowed around a sudden lump in her throat. "Sugarsnap. We're *barely* eighteen. What are you, pregnant?"

Ivy giggled, and gratefulness washed over Frankie in an overwhelming wave. All of this—Bulldeen, resurrection, manslaughter, and judging whispers—was worth it if she got to have Ivy Wexler with a skull ring on her finger and black lace around her neck.

"New York," Ivy whispered.

"New York," Frankie replied, kissing her shoulder right over the scar.

She left Ivy's house that night walking on air. Two weeks. No school, no half-empty hallways getting even more empty when Frankie and Ivy walked in. Just two boredom-filled weeks of working every day at the bakery, and then they were *out* of there. Her and Ivy and KJ crossing state lines into their new lives, never to darken Bulldeen's door again.

It was a short walk back to her house. Halfway there, she started humming. She'd go home, do her washing. Figure out what to pack and what to throw out. Clean the dishes piling up in the sink—her mom was home a lot more since her dad moved out of town, which was surprisingly nice when she wasn't wasted, but she never cleaned her dishes. So unless Frankie wanted to start eating noodles out of mugs, she had to do them. Then again, her mom had congratulated her this morning about her last ever day of school, so maybe she'd go the extra mile and do a congratulatory washing up—

Something exploded at the back of her head.

Her knees slammed into the ground, then her hands. That terrible pain was a switch turning everything off: sight fuzzing around the edges, motor functions failing.

Someone was behind her. Frankie tried turning to see them, but instead her face hit the yellow grass. A stone dug into her cheek. It stung.

Kiss it better, Frankie thought, dazed. *Ivy*—

Everything   went   dark.

chapter two

It was dark.

Frankie frowned. Dry grass crunched under her face. Her head felt like a bruised fruit, but when she reached back and felt at her skull, everything was intact. The skin wasn't even broken.

She sat up, groaning. She reached to pick the pebble out of her cheek and gasped as sharp pain flared up her arm. The moonlight revealed a red gash in the crook of her elbow. She stared at it. Blood dripped onto her tights.

"Shit," Frankie slurred. Her tongue was heavy. She tried again, and this time it came out normally. "Shit."

She checked her skirt pocket. Her pocketknife was still there, unopened and unbloodied. *Good news,* she imagined telling Ivy, *I'm not kidnapped. Bad news: somebody knocked me out and cut my arm and then just…left me here?* Frankie pressed a hand over her wound and hissed as the dripping stopped. If somebody wanted to intimidate her, wouldn't they have left a note? Dragged her someplace? Beat her up? Knocking her out and cutting her arm felt like a bizarre way for someone to tell her to leave town.

"I'm leaving in two weeks," Frankie declared to the empty neighborhood. "This was totally unnecessary!"

No answer. She wobbled to her feet. She should go home and get her mom to clean her up.

Frankie stood and imagined her mom awkwardly tying a bandage, offering to watch TV with her, offering a grudging ride to the emergency room and being relieved when Frankie turned her down.

She turned around and walked back to Ivy's.

Ivy's parents wanted to call the police.

"No cops," Frankie insisted. Kate Higgins, the old police chief, was long gone. The new chief, Lissiter, was nice. But a nice cop was still a cop. "They'd probably give the guy a pat on the back, anyway."

"That's not funny," Ivy snapped, glowering across the kitchen table.

"I'm not laughing." Frankie resisted the urge to reach over and smooth out the worry line between Ivy's brows. She punched her shoulder instead. "Hey, I'm *fine*. I have a headache and a little baby cut on my arm—"

"A *big* cut."

"I don't even need to go to hospital!"

The Wexlers traded a dubious look.

"I *don't*," Frankie repeated. She rotated her injured arm. Her inner elbow twinged under the bandage. It probably did need stitches, but it was an hour's drive to the nearest hospital and Frankie would rather have a scar. She didn't want more questions, didn't want nurses' wary glares, didn't want the Wexlers to call her mom. She just wanted to climb into bed next to Ivy (they could get away with ditching the sleeping bag if one of them had been through a Traumatic Event) and hold her until she fell asleep.

Ivy's mom tutted. "I can't believe someone would want to do this to you. You're odd, to be sure, but you're harmless!"

Harmless. A lump formed in Frankie's throat, remembering a creature that used to be April biting a chunk out of Ivy's arm, sinking her teeth into KJ's ankle. Chewing on the exposed meat of Marvin's brain as he twitched and screamed and finally stilled.

"Weird hazing," Frankie said, watching Ivy's parents head to the other room to call her mom. Letting her know her daughter was okay, and that she was staying over for the millionth time. Like Frankie's mom would care.

"Another reason on the endless list of why we need to—" Frankie stopped. Ivy was staring at her, eyes wide and fearful.

"Whoa, hey, what?"

11

Ivy hesitated. "Remember that movie we watched last week?"

It was hard to focus over the pounding in her head. "Uh. *Dead Gore*?"

"They needed a power source," Ivy said. "So they took some of the girl's…blood."

"Yeah," Frankie said, head still throbbing. "Why…"

Ivy touched her bandaged elbow.

It still took a second. A laugh shivered up her throat. "This isn't—this isn't that. This isn't *Bulldeen* shit. This is just…"

A strange sense of déjà vu trembled in her stomach. They'd done this before, back in a school bathroom, Ivy freaking out over the renewing thornfruit and Frankie lying through her teeth, trying to convince her it was all okay.

"This is some weirdo who wanted to screw with me before I got the hell out of town," Frankie croaked. *Please, god, let it be true.*

"Then why cut you? Why—"

"I don't know how these guys get their kicks!" Frankie grabbed her hands. The low murmurs of the Wexlers drifted in from the next room. "It's not *magic*, Ives. It's just assholes."

She squeezed Ivy's hand. Ivy squeezed back, but it was clear she didn't believe it. Not entirely. Did she have that same déjà vu Frankie was trying so desperately to ignore?

Frankie sighed. "Do you want KJ to come over?"

"Movie night?" Ivy's smile was thin. KJ was the only other person in town who knew about this stuff. The full story. As full as Ivy and Frankie knew it, anyway.

Frankie nodded.

Ivy sighed, pretending to think it over. "Fine. But only if we get to cuddle after my parents go to bed."

"Done." Frankie checked the kitchen doorway. Nobody there. She ducked in and stole a kiss, and when she pulled back, Ivy's smile was almost solid.

KJ oozed cool. Effortless. Handsome without trying too hard. To anyone else, he took the news of his good friend's attack with a barely raised eyebrow and a: *I guess the last day of school congratulations are on hold.* Ivy's parents didn't notice the hands he slipped into his hoodie pockets, drumming up a storm where nobody could see.

His hands were still in his pockets when they sunk onto the couch to watch *Charlie's Angels.*

"Soooo," he said, looking determinedly at a man flinging himself off a boat because of Drew Barrymore. "Haven't heard anything about thornfruit growing in. That's good."

Ivy sent Frankie a pointed look. Frankie ignored it.

"That's not what this is," Frankie said.

"Uh-huh," KJ muttered. "Hope not."

Ivy held out a bowl of microwave popcorn across the couch. KJ shook his head. His hands were still buried in his pockets. Frankie watched the fabric twitch, impossible to catch unless you were already looking.

They made it another two minutes before KJ sucked in a breath.

"I know we don't talk about it," he blurted, "But I was looking into those cannibal murders in LA."

"Don't," Frankie warned. Beside her, Ivy was tense. This, they could agree on.

"I'm just saying, the Dead Freaks moved there and then the very next *year*—"

"It has nothing to do with us!"

"We don't need to know," Ivy added, hand entwining tightly with Frankie's, a salty touchstone to focus on instead of the crap KJ was spouting.

KJ sat back against the couch, mouth pulled tight against the things he wasn't saying. There was more to the story. Frankie knew that. Something had happened to former police chief Kate Higgins; Frankie had overheard a customer at the bakery whispering about it to his wife. During the LA cannibal murders Kate had gone out to join the Dead Freaks, just for a visit, and then...

And then something bad happened. Frankie didn't know how bad, and she didn't want to know. She didn't make eye contact once with the rest of the Higgenses before they left town, and whenever gossip came up, she avoided it. It was surprisingly easy. Nobody wanted to talk to her.

"Maybe this kind of thing—" KJ swallowed. "Once it starts...it doesn't stop."

Frankie shook her head. "No. That's not how it works. They must've done something, in LA. Ivy did something with Babylove, and then I did something with April, and...and we didn't DO anything, this time. So nothing's happening."

She stared at him pleadingly. KJ opened his mouth, and Frankie braced herself for the obvious counterargument: *just because you didn't do anything, doesn't mean someone else didn't.*

But KJ was an expert at avoidance. He said it himself sometimes, always with a self-deprecating chuckle. *Avoid and deny—the KJ Duong special.*

KJ sagged back into the couch. "If you say so."

He pulled his feet up. Frankie turned back to the screen and pretended not to notice his fingers rubbing a soothing circle over his scarred ankle.

chapter three

Jobs were thin on the ground in Bulldeen, even if you weren't pariahs. Frankie and Ivy had been planning on taking a loan from Ivy's parents when a miracle happened: Hockstetter choked to death on his own vomit in the kitchen of his bakery. His son, Grady, moved back from Missouri two weeks later to take over. It was the stupidest thing he could've done—who moved back to a dying town to take over a subpar bakery?—but Grady wasn't caught up on the town gossip, which meant that when Frankie bolted in on the first day to offer her services behind the counter, Grady didn't laugh her out of the bakery.

Keep your hair tied back and don't drip mascara on the scones and you've got a job, he'd said. It paid less than minimum wage and Frankie had to work both weekend days, but it meant she had savings. Plus he agreed to let her work every day between classes ending and graduation.

The telltale sounds of a whisk drifted to the front of the bakery when Frankie arrived on Saturday morning. Grady let Chief Lissiter come in early on the weekends to bake. *Stress relief,* he called it. He didn't even get paid.

Frankie didn't bother going out back to say hi. Like the rest of the town, Lissiter didn't want to talk to her. He'd say hi if he saw her, always with a strained, brief smile, and then go back to what he was doing. If there was nothing to do, he'd invent something.

So she was surprised when he emerged from the back room in an apron, smiled his usual strained smile, and then didn't get out of there as soon as he got a Coke from the fridge.

"What happened there?" He pointed at the bandage around her arm.

Frankie emptied a roll of coins into the till, ignoring the throb that echoed through her head at the clanging noise. "My heroin habit is taking its toll."

He laughed nervously. Frankie waited for him to disappear back to the kitchen, but he hovered awkwardly in the doorway instead.

"Heading out of town after you graduate?"

Frankie snorted. "Isn't everybody? There's nothing *here*. Everything's closing down. Surprised this place is still open."

"Gotta have your morning coffee, I guess." He took a hasty sip of Coke. He still didn't meet her eyes, watching the till, the stained linoleum, anything but her. "Where you headed?"

Frankie slammed the till closed, treasuring Lissiter's wince at the loud noise. "New York."

"City?"

"'Course."

"Hope it treats you right." He tilted the Coke toward her, a mini-salute, and backed through the door.

Frankie chewed her tongue. She'd seen the guy every weekend for the last four months and this was the first conversation she'd had with him. Her dyed hair made him uncomfortable even before the black magic rumors. But he didn't want anything bad to happen to her, she was pretty sure. He just wanted her to stay the hell away from him.

She waited until he was tucked into the back room, the metallic swish of the whisk resuming. "Are you getting out?"

The whisk paused. The bakery was silent long enough she wondered if she was being ignored. Then Lissiter called, "Getting out isn't that simple. I've lived here all my life."

So have I. Frankie kept it behind her teeth.

The whisk started up again. Frankie's head pounded. She felt the back of her head, the tender spot that had reminded her of bruised fruit. Not even a scab to prove it. By the time her arm healed, she'd be in New York. Another life. People wouldn't cringe away from her in the street, wouldn't glare at

16

her while she shopped, wouldn't hiss *witch* or *dyke* at her as she passed. Just two weeks and none of this Bulldeen shit would touch her again.

The bell over the door chimed.

Frankie cursed herself for not locking it after she came in. "We open in five minutes." She looked up.

Ivy stood in front of the till, face shining with sweat, chest heaving.

"Shit, sugar—" Frankie bit her cheek before the word could finish. She ducked out from behind the counter, lowering her voice. "What *happened?*"

Ivy shook her head, dazed. "What's...what's the thing you put over someone's face and they pass out?"

"Uh. Chloroform?"

"I think someone just chloroformed me."

"*What?*"

Ivy shushed her.

Frankie's hands twitched to reach up, brush away Ivy's sweaty hair from her forehead. But Lissiter was in the kitchen, and the bakery windows were wide.

Ivy held up her left arm. A deep cut was in the crook of her unscarred elbow, leaking blood onto the linoleum.

"Jesus." Frankie grabbed napkins from the dispenser and packed them to the wound, apologizing when Ivy hissed. "Sorry."

"It was a woman," Ivy whispered. "I saw a bracelet."

"Did you recognize it?"

"It had a dog charm on it? I think?" Ivy's lip trembled, eyes wide with fear and that creeping dread that Frankie had been fighting down since Ivy said *remember that movie we watched last week?* How many times had they clung to each other, promising each other it was over?

"Hey." Frankie held Ivy's arm with both hands, a solid press against the napkins as they soaked up the blood. She tried for an encouraging smile. "We'll handle this, alright? Whatever this is, we'll figure it out, and then we're out of

17

town. *New York, New York.* The city never sleeps, and no one spits at us in the street or steals our blood for dark magic."

Ivy's laugh was high pitched and flimsy. She rubbed her face, smearing red across her cheek. "Why knock you out and chloroform me?"

"They're getting smarter?" Frankie grabbed another napkin and dabbed at the blood Ivy just trailed over her face. "Maybe don't touch your face while your hand's bloody, alright?"

"Oh." Ivy stared at the bloody napkin Frankie was holding, her face twisting in disgust. "Ew."

A loud clang from the kitchen. Frankie turned, but the doorway was still clear. If they were lucky, Lissiter would be too busy swinging baking equipment around to hear them.

"You should go get this cleaned up," Frankie said, turning back. "It looks…Ivy?"

Ivy was still staring at the bloody napkin, her gaze strangely distant. For a moment her eyes looked almost black. Then she looked up and her eyes were their usual cornflower blue.

A trick of the light, Frankie told herself, stomach twisting uneasily.

Ivy rubbed her forehead. "Maybe we should get out of here. Just…forget about graduation and your two-week notice."

Frankie laughed, loud and panicked, in case Lissiter was listening in. The last thing she needed was a cop reporting them back to her boss. Grady wasn't a complete sack of shit, but she didn't know for sure if he'd kick her out if she joked about ditching her job.

"I need this last paycheck," Frankie whispered. "And your parents will kill us if they don't get graduation pictures."

Ivy groaned and kneaded again at her head, skin going white where her fingers were digging in. "I know. I just…I want this to be over. I want New York. I want a double bed and I want to hold your goddamn *hand*. On the *street*."

"Kinky." Frankie grinned, warmth seeping through the desperation. She plucked Ivy's hands away from her head, bloody napkin crumpled between them. "We'll figure this out, sugarsnap. Alright? We'll just…be careful. Stick together. Start carrying mace. Though if my pocketknife was this *useless,* we might as well forget mace…"

She trailed off. Ivy's gaze had gone distant again, her hands slack in Frankie's grip. Her head lolled downwards.

"Ivy?" Worry curdled in Frankie's gut. Was she having a seizure? Could chloroform do that? Frankie reached for her chin. "Hey—"

Ivy grabbed her wrists. Frankie let out a pained gasp at the unrelenting grip.

"Ives," Frankie said through gritted teeth. "What's—"

Ivy's head snapped up. Her eyes were black. No trick of the light this time, just strange, wet black taking over her eyes. Dark vines crept out onto her cheeks. Tendrils sunk into her jaw. Taking *root.*

Pain bit into Frankie's wrists. Ivy's nails were digging in. One hand had red nails, one had black. Frankie had touched them up last night, sliding a coat of clear gloss on top while KJ snored on the couch beside them.

Ivy's lips peeled back in a snarl. Her jaw jerked, slow and halting, like a puppet with not enough strings, like April on fire on the gym floorboards, trying to speak through the thing holding her hostage.

"*I'll—get—her—back,*" Ivy spat, and the voice was not the rasp of the creature that had spoken to them twice before, nor was it Ivy's voice put through a shredder. This voice was familiar. Entitled. *Spiteful.* Frankie hadn't heard it since Homecoming when she was being pushed back against the mirrors.

"Marvin," Frankie whispered.

19

Marvin-Ivy's mouth flinched into a grin. Blood dripped from her nose, over her bared teeth.

Frankie felt her own mouth open. She wasn't sure what she was going to say—*get out of her* or *how dare you* or *won't you just stay dead, you annoying SHIT*—but before she could get anything out, Ivy went limp, hands dropping from Frankie's wrists.

Heavy footsteps from the kitchen. "Think that should be it for today."

Ivy wobbled.

"Oh shit." Frankie's arms came up, but it was too late. Lissiter walked in—eyes on the floor as they usually were around Frankie, as if trying not to be ensnared by her witchy gaze—just as Ivy slipped through Frankie's shaky grip and collapsed on the floor in a crumpled, twitchy heap.

chapter four

"I'm fine," Ivy mumbled, as Frankie propped her up against a shelf of cold dough.

Frankie laughed shakily. "How the tables turn!"

The walk-in fridge was narrow and cramped and stunk of rot. They'd had to wedge a carton of milk in the door to stop it from closing—the handle didn't work from the inside.

Frankie cocked her head, listening. Faint sounds of the till opening and closing came from the front room. Lissiter had helped lug Ivy into the walk-in fridge, then ducked out front to open the store. He hadn't met either of their eyes the whole time, even as he'd mumbled something about calling an ambulance, or somebody's parents. He'd seemed relieved when they turned him down.

Frankie held yet another napkin to Ivy's nose. "Lean forward, princess."

Ivy gave her a knowing look—*going back to old pet names?*—but tilted her head forward obediently. Blood soaked into the tissue-thin paper.

Frankie watched Ivy breathe. Black stripe in her blonde hair. Pitted scars in one arm, a cut in another. A skull ring on her finger, a dark ribbon around her neck, blood streaking a pair of black tights she borrowed from Frankie. This Ivy was so different to the cheerleader who had sauntered up to Frankie's cafeteria table all those years ago, and Frankie couldn't decide if the lurch in her stomach was pride or sorrow. What dark shit had they fallen into this time?

Ivy spoke, muffled by the napkins. "I think it's stopped."

Frankie pulled the wad away. Red stained Ivy's nostrils and upper lip, tracking down her chin. But the flow had stopped.

"Okay," Frankie said. "Okay. So—"

"I was somewhere dark." Ivy's lashes fluttered. Frankie flinched, but Ivy's eyes stayed their usual blue. No liquid black, no tendrils creeping out to her cheeks.

"What did I—" Ivy rubbed her forehead. "Did I say something? When I was...out?"

"You said, uh. You said *I'll get her back.*" Frankie laughed again, a thread of hysteria leaking in. She tried to smile. Make this a little less scary. "It was—it sounded like Marvin."

Ivy sucked in a breath. Not surprise. Just dread. And...guilt?

"*Ivy,*" Frankie snapped, voice so forceful Ivy jolted up. Her head bounced against the metal shelf behind her, only slightly cushioned by a cheese wheel.

Frankie winced. "Shit, sorry. Ives, you didn't *do* anything, right?"

"No! God, why would I—" Ivy gave her such an annoyed look Frankie had to fight a genuine laugh. "Something happened last year. Nothing like *this*, just...before Marvin's parents moved away, his mom kind of...showed up outside my house? And grabbed me while I was taking the trash out?"

Frankie stared at her.

"I know," Ivy said.

Frankie groaned, dropping her head against Ivy's shoulder.

"I *know,*" Ivy whispered, hand coming up to comb through Frankie's dark hair, automatic as breathing. "I didn't think—"

Frankie pulled back despairingly. "What *happened*?"

"Nothing. She just grabbed me. Said..." Ivy bit her lip. Her voice trembled. "She said I did something to her son."

Frankie shivered. It had nothing to do with the fridge and everything to do with the memory that would never leave her: Ivy in her Homecoming dress, red and blazing, shoving Marvin with all her strength. Marvin skidding on the blood-soaked bathroom floor. The impossibly loud *crack* of his head meeting the sink. A chunk of porcelain beside his trembling head. The exposed white of his skull. A monster in April's skin bent over the jelly of his brain, mouth open—

A heavy knock made them jolt. Ivy scrubbed a tear from her cheek, Frankie wiping hurriedly at the remaining blood on her face.

Lissiter stood in the gap in the door, averting his gaze. "Uh, you girls alright in there?"

"Yes," they chorused.

Lissiter hesitated. "Sure you don't want me to call somebody's folks?"

"Yes!"

"Alright." Lissiter shuffled his feet, heavy boots against scuffed linoleum.

A call rang out from the front. "*Hello? Are you open?*" It was barmy Mrs. McKay. Frankie ached for New York, where she couldn't identify everyone by voice alone.

"Well, I better…" Lissiter trailed off.

Frankie watched his boots vanish from view and let out a sigh of relief. "Marvin's parents split up, right? The dad's in, like, Hawaii? With a new wife?"

"I heard it was Michigan."

"Hope it's Hawaii. More glamorous." Frankie reached up and broke a hunk of cheese from the cheese wheel behind Ivy's head. "For your blood sugar."

Ivy opened her mouth.

Frankie slid the cheese in. "Did Marvin's mom wear a charm bracelet with a dog on it?"

Ivy shook her head, chewing tiredly. "Not a dog. It was a lion. I should've realized, I had dinner with them like eight times, everything was just so fuzzy—they were always going on about how the Martins were the kings of the jungle."

Frankie held out another piece of cheese. Ivy ate it off her fingers. Her lips were chapped and covered in drying blood.

Frankie brushed the red flecks off on her tights. "Do lions actually live in jungles?"

Ivy snorted. "No."

She gave Frankie the dry look she reserved for when people were being stupid, the one that meant they'd laugh about this later, and for a moment Frankie wasn't afraid at all. They'd done this twice before. They were so close to getting out of here. What was one more horror?

Then Ivy's eyelids fluttered and the fear swarmed back, thick and choking.

Frankie waited until those eyes, beloved and blue, were back on hers. She held out a hand.

"Come on," she whispered. "Back into the jungle."

They left Lissiter behind the counter with the keys to the safe and a promise that Frankie would be here the whole day tomorrow.

"I'll call Grady," Frankie told him. "Tell him he's gotta pay you for today."

"It's fine," Lissiter said after a long pause. Frankie couldn't tell if he was actually busy with the coffee machine or if he just didn't want to look at her. The last customer had left the shop, so she was betting on the latter.

He glanced up, eyeing the hasty bandage napkin around Ivy's arm, then the proper bandage around Frankie's. His eyebrows creased.

"Uh," he said. His jaw snapped shut and he bent over the coffee machine like he wanted to meld into the metal. "Bye."

"Bye," Frankie muttered, heart pounding in her chest. She hadn't even considered how it would look, her and Ivy with matching wounds at the same time. She could already hear the gossip brewing.

Twin bandages on their arms...what are they planning? Blood rituals? Will someone else die before they leave town?

Frankie was so busy rushing Ivy out of the bakery she didn't notice the people out front until it was too late.

24

"We don't need you around," Mrs. McKay was saying to a large, disheveled man in a dark hood. "Cluttering up the—oh!" Her croaks cut off as Frankie shoved the door open, clipping her stooped back.

"Jesus," Frankie blurted. "Sorry, Mrs. McKay."

Ivy reached out to steady the old woman, who turned to stare at them. Mrs. McKay's eyes were bleary with cataracts, her hands trembling around her cane. She looked at the girls like she didn't quite remember where she knew them from.

"That's quite alright, dears," she said, smiling thinly. Then she turned back to the hooded man and her smile sloughed away. "I did hope you'd left. Always haunting that Shop N' Save, bothering our good townsfolk."

Frankie paused. Mrs. McKay must've thought this guy was Leroy Child, the homeless man who had always hung around the Shop N' Save before his untimely death a few years back. Wild dogs, the police said. But everyone knew better. Leroy Child's torn up body was found just after Babe Simmons rose from the dead. The first official casualty of the Zombabedisaster—but not the last.

The disheveled man didn't speak. He was only a little taller than Frankie, and although his clothes were moth-eaten, his boots were strangely clean. His hood hung so far over his face Frankie couldn't see his eyes. Above his sweating chin, his thin lips pressed together into a white line that made Frankie think of scars.

"It was nice," Mrs. McKay continued. "Not having you around. It was…quieter."

Frankie shot a look at Ivy. Ivy raised her brows back. They turned as one.

"Hey," Frankie said. "Lay off."

The man's hood twitched toward them. A line of sweat dripped off his face.

Mrs. McKay took a moment to realize she was being spoken to. "Pardon me?"

Frankie lifted her chin. "Lay. *Off.*"

25

"He's just living his life," Ivy added. "Leave him be."

Mrs. McKay gaped. "Well," she croaked. "*Well*. I…"

Confusion clouded her hazy eyes. Her face went slack. She turned again, and seemed surprised to see the man standing in front of her. She peered at his hood, and her face melted into a shocked smile.

"Oh! You're back. I thought you were gone for good. Isn't this nice?" She gave his arm a pat and tottered off, cane unsteady on the cracked sidewalk.

"Sorry about her," Frankie said. "You, um…You'd have better luck outside the Shop N' Save."

He didn't reply, just turned his head back toward the asphalt. For a second Frankie wondered if she'd messed up— maybe Mrs. McKay had the whole situation wrong and he wasn't even homeless. His shoes *were* really nice—but then that thin, sweaty mouth opened.

"Thanks," he said, barely a mumble. He sounded confused. Like he hadn't expected that.

Frankie shrugged, wincing when it tugged at the cut on her arm. "No problem, man."

Something wet dripped down her fingers. Frankie looked down to see a line of blood over her hand where it was holding Ivy's arm. Blood seeped through the napkin bandages.

"Ew," Ivy whispered.

Frankie nodded. "Uh, sorry," she said to the hooded man. "We gotta—"

He cut her off. "You're nicer than they say."

Frankie stopped. He still wouldn't look at them, but it didn't sound…aggressive. No hidden insult, no secret warning. Still: a stranger rolls into their dying town the same week they both get attacked? She should be suspicious. You had to be suspicious of everyone in this damn town.

Frankie forced a smile, showing every single one of her teeth. Just in case. She was aiming for threatening, but she was tired and her head still hurt and her arm ached and her girlfriend was leaning on her, sweat saturating Frankie's clothes. It was hard to look anything but exhausted.

"Yeah," Frankie said. "Don't believe everything they say in Bulldeen."

The back of her neck prickled all the way down the street, Ivy's arm heavy around her shoulders. But when she turned, the street was empty.

chapter five

"So," KJ said the next day. "When you say *possessed*—"

Frankie shushed him. They were almost inside the library, where the slightest whisper carried for miles.

She pushed the heavy library door open. The AC blew lukewarm air in their faces. KJ tugged on the thick collar of his work shirt. He used to change into a hoodie on breaks, but the girls hadn't given him time to do anything other than follow them out of the Shop N' Save and down the road to the library.

We're on a time limit, Frankie had told him. She meant their lunch breaks. Mostly.

Next to her, Ivy twitched. She was still sweating, a fine sheen that wouldn't go away even after cold showers.

KJ eyed her. The sweating didn't freak him out, he insisted when they came to get him on his lunch break. The twitching *definitely* did.

"You good?"

Ivy swallowed. "I'm great."

"Great," KJ muttered, and waved at the stacks. "Guide us to the dark books, you witchy weirdos."

The library was empty apart from Miss Henrietta, the only librarian employed by the town council, who should not have chosen a career that involved talking to people. Her mouth was naturally pinched, and it only pinched further as she looked up from her book and saw who it was.

Frankie nodded at her. Miss Henrietta slouched down further behind her desk and glowered, her typical reaction to Frankie even before the dark magic/probable lesbian rumors started.

"Old friends," Frankie whispered as they approached the dusty *occult* section she'd frequented when she was helping Ivy out with the Babylove business years ago. Most of the

28

section was bullshit, all horoscopes and hauntings and hexes. The only helpful book was a history one detailing the crimes of women who were put to death in the Salem witch trials, and even most of that was crap.

Frankie heaved the book off the shelf and sat down, setting it open on the worn carpet. "I don't know how much it'll be about dispelling…cleansing…stuff," she said as Ivy sank down beside her. "It gets pretty Christian later on. Think it'll be mostly, like, repenting. Sign of the cross. Angel shit."

KJ nudged the book with his pristine sneaker. "I mean. Have you *tried* that?"

The girls glared up at him.

"Alright," KJ muttered, and got down on the ground with them.

Frankie passed him a tiny guide to spellcasting.

He took it, pushing his hair away from his face. He'd let it grow long this past year. "How do we know what's real and what's bullshit?"

"Most of it is bullshit," Frankie told him. "It's like…it's like there are all these stories, and maybe they have *something* true in them but it's so shrouded in crap it might as well be nothing. Remember that nixing spell we spent weeks chasing?"

Ivy snorted. "Hey, maybe it exists. Maybe we just couldn't find it."

An ashy cough echoed down the aisle. Frankie twisted to see Janitor Larry freezing in mid-step, gaunt and creepy in his grimy jumpsuit, gripping a broom.

"Uh." The broom jerked in his hands, scraping against the carpet before he seemed to realize what a bad alibi that was. He took a step away from the aisle.

"Hey," Frankie barked. She waved over the occult section. "Anyone else look through these?"

Janitor Larry froze, his escape foiled. "Can't remember."

"Homeless guy? Big hood?"

29

Janitor Larry frowned, turning back enough for Frankie to glimpse his confusion. "What?"

She waved the question away. "What about Karin Martin? Marvin's mom?"

Janitor Larry hunched into his bony shoulders. "Can't remember," he mumbled, and rushed off faster than she'd ever seen him move.

"Homeless guy?" KJ repeated as Janitor Larry vanished from the aisle.

"Keeping our options open," Frankie told him. "Has he been outside the Shop N' Save?"

"No. We haven't had a regular since Leroy got ripped to bits."

A hiss echoed from the other side of the aisle. Frankie looked up to see Miss Henrietta, two angry spots glowing on each cheek.

"Out," she instructed.

Frankie raised her hands. "We weren't doing anything!"

"You're—loud." Miss Henrietta's gaze darted to the books splayed out on the floor. Fear flickered over her face, and Frankie's stomach turned sour at yet another reminder of how *terrifying* they were to the rest of Bulldeen, all these people they saw every day, the people they'd grown up with. Miss Henrietta had chastised Ivy and Frankie as children, wiping their fingerprints off picture books. Janitor Larry had probably stepped around them as toddlers. And here they were, wide-eyed in terror at the goth and her corrupted cheerleader.

Miss Henrietta swallowed. The fear was gone, replaced by that righteous rage.

"*Out*," she spat, and the teenagers were on their feet before the word was out of her venomous mouth.

"I can't wait to never see her again," Ivy announced as they headed outside. "I wish—*ow*."

Frankie caught her elbow. They were just outside the library doors, the midday sun harsh on their scalps. "You okay?"

Ivy gave her a weak thumbs-up. "Just…bright."

Frankie held up her hands, shielding her from the sun. Ivy laughed, tight but real.

KJ sauntered up with the kick in his step he put in when he was trying to be funny. Letting go of his Cool Guy Persona a little. It happened more and more since he graduated high school.

"Look what I gooot," he sing-songed, and pulled out a book out of his thick work shirt. It was the tiny spellcasting guide, the front cover bent from its hasty jailbreak.

Frankie tweaked the bent cover. "She'll have your head for that."

"Follow you to New York," Ivy said quietly, kneading her temple. "Hunt you down."

Frankie resumed her sun shield. Ivy talking so quietly had to mean the headache was a big one. Last night she'd winced when her parents talked above a whisper. They had to go to another room when they microwaved popcorn.

Ivy reached up and clasped Frankie's shielding hand. Frankie glanced around—someone's parent on the other side of the street, the dressmaker further up the road. No one was looking, but that didn't mean they couldn't see them out of the corner of their eye. Or someone wouldn't drive past and see them out their window. Or someone wasn't standing in a dark shop window somewhere, watching them with disgust.

"I need to go home," Ivy said, face still creased with pain. "You two need to go back to work."

KJ sighed, shoving the book back down his work shirt.

"I'll take you home," Frankie offered.

"You already walked out of one shift."

"You sure?"

"I'm fine." Ivy kneaded her temples, smiling tightly. "Go on. I'll see you at home." She scratched a spot next to her mouth where a worry scab once bloomed. The skin was already red under her nails.

Frankie caught her hand. "Hey. I thought we were done with that."

"It's never *done*." Ivy's hand flexed in her grip, trying to scratch the reddened spot that had taken weeks to heal over. "It just...stops. For a while. Until next time."

KJ whistled, several paces down. He wavered on the spot, waiting for Frankie to catch up. They had about a block before the supermarket came up and he had to peel off.

Ivy squeezed her hand. "I'll see you at my house."

Frankie thought about Ivy's scratching for the rest of her shift. That nervous tic came up sometimes, of course, but never enough to cause damage. Not since the Babylove weeks. The way this was going—magic shit starting up again with no end in sight—she'd scratch that spot to the blood in no time. Start picking at her hands. Bite chunks out of her cuticles.

The bell over the door chimed. Frankie blinked and realized she'd been drawing a circle into the countertop with a toothpick. Oops.

"Hiya." The homeless man from before waved at her, hood obscuring half his face despite the summer heat.

Frankie's nerves ratcheted up to eleven. Did he know she'd been asking about him? No, it had been barely a few hours since they asked Janitor Larry. He wouldn't just...run over and tattle, would he? Did these guys even know each other?

"Hi," Frankie blurted, realizing he was waiting for a response. "What can I get you?"

"Uh," he said. He coughed, then his voice became strangely nasal. "The...banana bread. Please."

Frankie bagged it. He handed her a fifty-dollar bill. Huh.

"Someone felt generous this morning," the man said, and coughed. His voice had lost its nasality for a second. "Sorry. Fighting off a cold."

"Sure," Frankie said. She felt guilty about being suspicious of him. Maybe he was just a harmless dude trying to get by.

He cleared his throat. "Saw you and your friend earlier."

Frankie's neck prickled. Screw this guy, something was *up*. Maybe Mrs. Martin hired him to scope her out, keep her updated on the Ivy situation? That would explain the fifty.

"She looked like she was having some trouble," the man continued. "Did she catch something, too?"

Frankie gritted her teeth. "Yeah. *Bad* cold."

"Sorry to hear it." The man wavered in place, clutching his bag of banana bread. "I—I wanted to thank you. For the other day. Didn't expect it from you."

Frankie picked the toothpick back up and imagined pulling the guy's hood off and driving it into his eye.

"Why?" she said flatly. "Been listening to Bulldeen gossip? Thought we'd be all…killing kittens and drinking baby blood? We're just a couple of teenagers trying to live their goddamn lives, dude."

"Right. No. Of course." He jerked like he was going to wipe his forehead, then remembered it was under a hood. "Sorry. Bye."

He rushed out. Frankie almost felt bad for him. She *would*, if she wasn't now eighty percent convinced he was part of the plot to possess her girlfriend. She twisted to watch him out the window, trying to see where he went. But the street was empty. He wasn't on the street or ducking into another shop. He was just…gone.

Ivy was asleep. Frankie tabled her "Mrs. Marvin's lackey" idea about the homeless man and climbed into Ivy's bed. She shuffled close to Ivy, looping her arms around her waist and breathing in the barely-there scent of Ivy's shampoo. She'd been skipping washes since the whole…possession thing.

I'm just too tired, Ivy told her yesterday, avoiding her eyes. Like Frankie was going to take her parents' side and hassle her about her oily hair. Like Frankie gave a shit.

33

Frankie would tell her about dry shampoo when she woke up. Dry shampoo and her Mrs. Martin lackey idea. Maybe they could chase down the guy and corner him, make him reveal Mrs. Martin's secrets. Then they'd track her down and force her to undo whatever they'd done to Ivy, banish Marvin's soul and get the hell out of town.

Frankie was half in a dream when Ivy stirred, twisting in her arms. Frankie felt a weight hovering over her and smiled.

"Hey," she murmured. "Was waiting for you to—"

Something dripped onto her forehead.

She opened her eyes. Ivy stared down at her, black eyes hard and vicious. Dark veins spidered into her cheeks, setting down poisonous roots. Blood dripped from her nose.

Frankie couldn't help it: her mouth opened. The scream was still forming when Ivy's hands closed around her neck.

chapter six

Frankie's scream died in her throat.

Ivy's fingers were iron. Frankie scrabbled at her wrists. Those fingers—*Marvin's* fingers?—only pressed harder. Frankie gasped for breath through her squeezed windpipe. Spots danced in the corners of her vision. A sharp burst of pain behind her eyes.

Ivy, Frankie mouthed. A tear slid down her cheek. *Ives—*

Marvin-Ivy's mouth twisted into a smug smile. Marvin Martin was insufferable, even in death, even wearing his ex-girlfriend's face. Frankie wanted to headbutt him, but the grip around her neck was too solid, the body on top of her pressing down too heavily.

Marvin-Ivy bent down to whisper in Frankie's ear. *"I— dreamed—of this."*

I could gouge out his eyes, Frankie thought deliriously. Then she imagined Ivy screaming, blood pouring from her ruined sockets. Would that be worse than Ivy waking up to find her girlfriend dead underneath her?

Frankie reached up, trembling with effort. She placed her weak hands on cheeks she'd stroked hundreds of times, fine bones where she'd pressed kisses. She couldn't do it. Could she? It wouldn't be that bad, Frankie thought. Dying like this. In those euphoric, hazy moments before the world went black—she could convince herself it was Ivy. Not bad, dying under someone you've loved so well.

Before she could reach the eyes, Marvin-Ivy pulled back, confusion and surprise warring on his borrowed face.

"What? But—" His grip loosened. Frankie managed a thimbleful of air.

Marvin-Ivy frowned, head cocking like he was listening to something far away. Confusion gave way to frustration.

"Fine," he growled. Marvin-Ivy leaned back down. *"Later."*

And then his hands went slack. Frankie gulped desperately and sat up, caught between pulling Ivy close and pushing her away. She coughed, a sob catching in her chest.

Ivy's head lolled on her shoulder. "Frankie...what..."

Frankie shook. Another cough. Another sob.

"Frankie—hey, what's wrong?" Ivy gasped, pulling in Frankie's face. "Your *eye*—"

"My *eye*?" Frankie stopped, bending into a full coughing fit. Great, was *she* possessed now? "What's wrong with my eye?" she rasped.

"You look like you burst a blood vessel."

Frankie sagged against her, relief washing over her in a wave. "Oh thank god."

"Your neck is red," Ivy said slowly. She wiped Frankie's tears away, horror seeping into her voice. "You have blood on your face. What happened? Did I—"

Frankie stumbled off the bed. "We need to go."

Ivy wavered, and Frankie watched the protestations swell: *but your job, but graduation, but my parents, but KJ—*

Another drop of blood fell from Ivy's nose. She wiped it away and stood.

"Where's my purse?"

They took Ivy's dad's car.

"We'll pay him back," Ivy insisted as they jerked out of the driveway. Their suitcases were in the back—Frankie had told Ivy about Marvin's promise of *later*. They didn't want to stick around a second longer than they had to.

"Or," Ivy started as they careened down Main Street, "we don't have to drive all the way to New York right now. We can just...go to another town and hide, and wait it out?"

Frankie shook her head, sweaty hands slipping against the steering wheel. "We don't know if Bulldeen's magic crap will follow us. It didn't leave the Dead Freaks alone in LA."

36

"Bulldeen can't be the only poisoned place in the world, maybe that was just them. Maybe those guys are poison." Ivy pulled the sunshade down.

"Are you—?"

"I'm fine." Ivy wiped sweat from her neck, blood from her chin. Her nose was still bleeding.

Frankie stepped harder on the accelerator. It was a short drive out of town. They were already approaching the town limits, the WELCOME TO BULLDEEN sign nailed back into place after someone had torn it off and beat the shit out of it years ago.

"We should call Kate," Ivy said. "Or Milly Hart."

The dented welcome sign glinted as they sailed past. If Frankie wasn't freaking out, she would have thought something cool, like *good riddance*. Or *see ya never*. As it was, her head was filled with a stream of *holy shit oh my goddamn shit*.

"We're so far over our heads," Ivy continued. She cupped her hand under her chin, catching the thin trail of blood still streaming down from her nose. "We have no idea what we're doing. We can't just go around asking about Mrs. Martin, no one will talk to us—"

"We're *out*," Frankie snapped. She waved at the barren fields where thornfruit used to grow, the stalks long rotted away. The fields stretched on for miles. She'd gotten lost in them when she was a kid, back when the plants loomed impossibly high. Her big sister had found her, after hours of wandering and crying out, convinced nobody would find her. She could still remember seeing her big sister April, who had to have been a kid herself at the time but looked impossibly grown up when she emerged from the stalks, scratched up and annoyed and *alive*, so alive, nobody would have ever guessed she'd be dead before she hit eighteen.

You little shit, April had said. *I've been looking everywhere.*

37

Frankie squeezed her eyes shut and then remembered *right, driving,* and wrenched them open. A long stretch of road lay ahead, completely empty. She could've spared a few more moments of closed eyes while she mourned her dead sister.

A low groan made Frankie jolt. It was so strange and guttural it took her a moment to realize it had come out of Ivy.

"Jesus, you scared me. What's—" Frankie froze.

Ivy curled over in her car seat, clutching her chest. Blood flowed down her chin. Another groan ripped up her throat, pained and desperate.

"Jesus," Frankie heard herself say. She stamped on the brake, and they careened to a lopsided stop on the side of the road. "Sugarsnap, sweetheart, holy shit, what do I *do*?"

A pained gasp wrenched up Ivy's throat. Her eyes were pried open, wet and pleading, but still blue. Still her Ivy.

"What's wrong?" Frankie croaked. "Everything's going to be okay—what do you need?"

Ivy's mouth gaped wordlessly. She pounded her chest, clutched her throat. She coughed. Blood splattered into her lap.

"Oh god," Frankie said. "Oh god, help…" She looked around. The road was still empty. No one for miles ahead. Behind them, the welcome sign loomed.

"I'll get help." Frankie pulled back into the street, twisting them back toward Bulldeen. She'd never done a U-turn before. Why had no one ever taught her how to do a damn U-turn?

Ivy writhed in the passenger's seat.

"You're okay," Frankie said as they sped back to town. "You're okay, everything's okay."

They careened past the dented welcome sign. Ivy uncoiled, gasping.

"What?" Frankie barked. "What's happening?"

38

Ivy wiped blood off her chin. "I think—I think I'm okay."

"Are you sure? Oh my god, what was *that*?"

Ivy shook her head. Winced at her lap, which was smeared with red. "I couldn't—my heart, it was—and I could hardly *breathe*, something was *yanking*, pulling me back—" She stopped. "Oh. Your neck."

"What?" Frankie felt it and hissed.

"It's bruised. It's so *bad*, Frankie." Ivy's lips trembled. Frankie reached out automatically, bringing up her sleeve to wipe at the stains on Ivy's face. They'd done this before, back at Homecoming. How many times would Frankie have to do this?

"I'm fine," Frankie told her. "Hey, no, come on, don't cry. It doesn't even hurt."

Ivy sobbed into her shoulder. Frankie held her, and if Ivy noticed wetness dripping onto her head, she didn't mention it.

"We shouldn't have let my parents talk us into staying for graduation," Ivy said, voice warped with tears. "Screw extra shifts, screw diplomas, screw photos. We should've got out the second we could."

The WELCOME TO BULLDEEN sign glinted behind them, menacing and loathsome. Frankie thought about ramming it with the car. Ever since Bulldeen's dark underbelly showed itself, Frankie had taken comfort in knowing they could leave. The second things got too much, they could light out of there. And now they were stuck. Locked in until this horror show ran its course.

Frankie pulled back to wipe some more at Ivy's face. It wasn't getting cleaner—it needed soap and water, not a dirty sleeve smearing the mess around. She moved her thumbs to the apples of Ivy's cheeks, where she'd pressed as Marvin was strangling her.

"I was going to gouge your eyes out," she admitted.

Ivy laughed wetly. "Atta girl."

39

"I didn't know what else to do."

"I wouldn't have been mad."

Frankie gave her a Look.

"Okay, I would've. My eyes are *gorgeous*. But I'd give them up if I got to keep you." Ivy pressed her mouth to Frankie's neck. "He can't have me," she whispered into the red ribbon Frankie had worn every day since that fateful Homecoming. "I'm yours."

Frankie kissed her. The back of her neck prickled, but she was too busy pressing kisses to Ivy's forehead, her nose, her mouth, to notice the homeless man standing stock-still behind the WELCOME sign, watching them with an unreadable   expression.

chapter seven

"We want to take her to a doctor."

Frankie sat up on the bed. Ivy's parents stood in the doorway in a tight huddle, clasping each other anxiously. It used to make Frankie uncomfortable how much they touched each other. Casual touches while doing the dishes, a kiss before leaving for work. It took a long time for her to recognize the uneasy twist in her gut as jealousy.

"She's not getting any better," Ivy's mom continued. "We just want to know if we should be worried."

"I'm fine," Ivy rasped, wobbling up from her pile of pillows. She pushed a sweaty strand of blonde hair off her forehead and smiled. "I just need to rest."

Ivy's parents exchanged a dubious look. Frankie didn't blame them. This wasn't *just a fever*, like they'd been insisting. Every time Frankie came over after work, they had another disturbing story. They'd never lead with it, of course. Frankie had to wheedle it out of them. It took several minutes of frantic subject changing—*we tried a new kind of chicken soup, how was the bakery*—for them to spill the beans.

Nosebleeds. Spitting up blood. Ivy was picking at her skin again, scabs sprouting along her hands and chin. She'd wake up screaming from nightmares she couldn't remember. She'd say strange things, insulting things, things Ivy would never say. Frankie was pretty sure her parents had gotten glimpses of black eyes, dark veins protruding from her cheeks, though they never said it like that. They said *can young people get cataracts* and *maybe blood poisoning*, all with that desperate tone all Bulldeen folk used when trying to convince themselves there was nothing dark and horrible on their doorstep.

Her voice gets weird sometimes, Ivy's dad whispered to her once, hands trembling around a cup of cocoa. *Like it isn't…hers.*

Frankie didn't know how they didn't recognize it. They'd had Marvin over for dinner enough to know his voice. It sounded different coming up Ivy's throat, but still…him. Marvin Martin in all his whining shithead glory.

"We just want a medical opinion," Ivy's mom said, staring worriedly at the bite scars on her daughter's arms. She often did this, as if afraid they'd multiply. She'd touch Ivy's arm during dinner and sigh *your perfect skin,* the same way she used to with the scabs Ivy picked on her face and hands. Ivy hated it. When Frankie got past the creepiness, she thought it was sweet. She liked it when parents gave a shit.

She glanced at the clock. Twenty minutes before she had to be at the bakery. "She doesn't need a doctor. She just needs rest."

"Seriously," Ivy said. "You try taking me to a doctor and I'll start screaming about the darkness again." She laughed hollowly.

Frankie gave her a look, but neither Ivy or her parents explained. Darkness?

Ivy winced. "Right. Bad joke."

"We just…" Ivy's dad said, and trailed off. He looked so helpless. Frankie ached for them, clutching each other like lost children.

Frankie squeezed Ivy's hand, pockmarked with scabs she'd been free of for years, and stood. "Okay, look."

Ivy tugged at her hand. "Frankie?"

"It's not a normal sickness," Frankie said. "Doctors won't be able to help. Someone is doing this to her—"

Ivy squeezed her hand in warning. "*Frankie.*"

"You gotta know something's wrong with this town," Frankie pleaded as Ivy's grip tightened. "You have to have heard whispers about Homecoming, about Babe Simmons, about all the horrible things that happened here. Bulldeen is

42

wrong, and it's poisoning her. We think Marvin's mom started it. She's back in town and she's used the town's bullshit to infect Ivy with, um, Marvin? And she might've gotten this homeless guy to help…"

Frankie trailed off, stomach sinking at the blank disbelief on their faces. When Frankie had found out the truth about Bulldeen's poisonous roots it felt like the wool had been pulled from her eyes. There was no wool with Ivy's parents, no sick suspicion finally clicking into place. They just stared.

Frankie grimaced. "I'm not explaining it right. So there's, like, this messed up well of dark power people can tap into, and I *think* it almost died with the thornfruit fields after the Dead Freaks left—"

"You must be very stressed," Ivy's mom said slowly. "With school ending, and working all those weekends, and now you're working every day before graduation."

"Scary things happen in this town," Ivy's dad said stiffly, like it hurt him to even say it. "I know it can be tempting to find something to make sense of it all—"

"Mom," Ivy said. "Dad. Come *on*."

"Marvin's mother—even if she could, she wouldn't make her *sick*." Ivy's mom laughed. "Karin is—she's a lovely woman. I should call her, actually. That horrible divorce, her husband running off to New Zealand with that new woman—"

"Jesus, fine, whatever." Frankie dug her palms into her eyes until she saw stars in the dark. "We're stressed. Sure. If you take her to the hospital her heart's going to give out the second you get past the town limits. Go for it."

Before she could think better of it, she bent down and pressed a kiss to Ivy's wrist, where a new scab was emerging. They'd trimmed Ivy's nails down to blunt crescents, but she still managed to pick to the blood.

"See you after work," Frankie said, and headed for the stairs. Her cheeks burned with embarrassment and worry and deep dread as Ivy's parents watched her descend the stairs.

Idiot, she scolded herself. Of course Ivy's parents wouldn't get it. What the hell was she thinking? And kissing Ivy's wrist in front of them—that was risky. They joked about how dense Ivy's parents were about this kind of thing, but they couldn't afford to be this obvious. Not now.

The phone rang. Frankie eyed it. She hadn't had to talk to a customer in an hour and she was hoping to keep it that way. But the phone kept ringing, and finally Frankie gave in.

"Hello this is Bull's Bakery, you're speaking to Frankie, how can I—"

"Your customer service voice sounds like a depressed robot." Even croaky, Ivy's voice was a breath of air after being underwater. Frankie couldn't stop her relieved laugh.

"That's the goal." She checked the windows. No one could hear her from the street, but try to tell her paranoia. Lissiter hadn't come by the past few days. They still had their regular deliveries, but people were already complaining about the lack of decent donuts.

"Did they try—"

Ivy cut her off. "Not today."

Figures. If Ivy's parents actually tried to take Ivy to the hospital, Frankie would've received a panicked call about how their daughter kept having heart attacks every time they got past town limits.

"I was thinking," Ivy started. "Remember what I said about calling Kate? Or Milly Hart? We should ask the Higgenses for their number. Or even Zombabe—I mean, Babe Simmons's dad, we could ask if he could get us in touch with Babe."

"What? Why would we—" Frankie rubbed her arms. Gooseflesh made her break out in shivery bumps. "Ivy, *no*."

"Why? Kate helped last time."

"I don't want…" Frankie chewed her tongue. "Nothing good happens around the Dead Freaks. You heard about LA, those cannibal murders."

44

"We don't know what actually happened. Maybe they weren't even involved."

"They started all this!"

"They didn't *start* this." Ivy coughed, voice thick and raspy. "The ritual was there before Babe got resurrected. They didn't start it, they just...kept it going. Like we did."

Frankie tasted copper in her mouth. After all this time talking Ivy out of picking her skin into scabs, Frankie had bit her tongue to the blood. The air trapped in the bakery was warm and stagnant, and still she shivered. Always summer, always blood, always strange voices beckoning from the dark. Wanting to feed. To *consume*.

"Is..." Frankie swallowed blood until she could only taste spit. "Is there a creature this time? Or just Marvin? Did you feel anything?"

Ivy was quiet for a long time. When she spoke it was hushed and horrified. "I think it...absorbed him. Or the other way around. If there's any thornfruit growing, it's so small no one's noticed. It's even weaker than last time. It's mostly Marvin, his...life force, or something, keeping it going. Like April."

"Okay. What does that mean?"

"I don't know," Ivy said. "I don't know how any of this shit works."

She sighed. Frankie pressed the phone into her cheek, pretending she felt the warmth of Ivy's sigh. Neither of them said anything: two scared girls not wanting to get eaten.

"I think we should talk to the Higginses," Ivy said finally. "Get Kate's number. It can't hurt."

"We don't..." Frankie chewed the inside of her mouth. "Shit. Alright, I'll go check them out after work."

"Great. I'll come along."

"Are you feeling—"

"I'll meet you at the bakery." Ivy coughed before she hung up. It was wet, something forcing up her throat. Frankie shivered, phone still pressed to her cheek, thinking of blood, black goo, sharp vines climbing out of Ivy's sweet mouth.

The Higgins vet clinic was closed. Not just closed—deserted. It had doubled as a vet clinic for longer than Frankie had been alive, and now it was gone just like most businesses in Bulldeen. When the thornfruit fields went, so did everything else. The only people left in town were the stubborn and the hopeless.

Frankie touched the spot where the HIGGINS VET CLINIC sign used to hang beside the front door. She'd gone down this street a dozen times in the last few months and she hadn't noticed.

"Could've at least boarded up the windows," Frankie said. "Made it more obvious."

Ivy didn't answer. She was still peering through the living room window, like it would reveal more than half-rotted boxes and dust bunnies. The Higginses were long gone. Still Ivy looked, pressing her forehead to the glass, leaving a smear of sweat. She'd looked so sick when she arrived at the bakery Frankie almost told her to go home. But Ivy had fixed her with a determined look that made Frankie swallow her protests and follow her out the door.

Frankie turned to a passerby walking their dog across the street. "Hey! When did the Higginses leave?"

The passerby, dress-shop owner Miss Petty, tightened her grip on her leash and kept walking without looking at them.

Frankie sighed. "Great. Thanks."

She turned back. Ivy was still peering through the abandoned window.

"Ivy?" Frankie hovered a hand over her shoulder.

Ivy twitched. Cold fear rose in Frankie's stomach, but when Ivy turned around her eyes were all blue.

"Babe Simmons's dad is gone too," Ivy said. "I checked on the way."

"Right. Well, there's gotta be *someone* we can ask."

Ivy shook her head. Her lips were a tight line, razor-sharp. "We shouldn't have left it so long."

She scratched a scab next to her mouth.

"Hey." Frankie caught her hand. Ivy stared at it, almost confused, like she didn't know why Frankie had stopped her.

Frankie tried to smile. "Let's go home."

Ivy nodded absently. Frankie dropped her hand. She didn't want to, but they were in public, and there was only so much hand-holding they could get away with.

KJ looked up from Ivy's bedroom floor. He was flipping through the stolen library book.

"Could've taken the bed," Ivy told him, climbing up onto it.

KJ shrugged. "Comfier down here."

"Sure," Frankie said, settling across Ivy's knees. "There's room up here for you, you know."

KJ waved her away. He'd been squirrelly around Ivy since the whole possession thing, and only more so now that Marvin was using Ivy to strangle Frankie and spit blood at her parents. Frankie didn't want to be pissed at him, but come on. *She* was the one who got strangled and *she* could still sit next to Ivy. It felt like a tiny betrayal, watching KJ sit on the floor pretending it wasn't killing his back.

"I tried to go back in to the library," KJ said. "But Miss Henrietta, uh. Chased me out."

Ivy sighed. "Did she give a reason?"

"Did she have to?" KJ flipped to a page and removed the broken rubber band he'd been using as a bookmark. "Anyway, you were right. Most of this is bullshit. But I've been *really* stretching, and here's what I got: Ivy's gotta stay connected to Ivy."

Frankie glanced over. Ivy looked just as unimpressed as she felt.

"That's not a fix," Frankie started, but KJ talked over her.

"Sure, but it's a *delay*. Ivy, you've been saying you feel more...*you* when Frankie's around. You don't get, uh, *episodes* in the mornings or the evenings when she's not at work. Or that one conversation with your dad when he told you about how he got fired as a teenager for drinking on the job."

Frankie laughed. "He *what*? *Your* dad?"

Ivy shrugged. "I like that story. He's got everything sorted, right? But he was such a mess when he was a teenager. It makes me, like…hopeful."

She smiled that small, pleased smile Frankie had barely seen in the past week. Frankie squeezed her hand, and the smile grew. For a moment some of the pallor faded from her cheeks, pink rushing back in.

KJ clapped loud enough to make them both jump. "There! That! It plugs Ivy back into herself."

"Not for long." Ivy's head sagged back into the pillow. "This doesn't bring us closer to getting him out of me."

KJ laid the rubber band back in place and closed the book. "I don't see you two coming up with ideas."

He rested his chin on the mattress. It made him look younger, like this was a sleepover in freshman year, and for a second Frankie mourned that it took them so long to find each other. They were right there, growing up in the same damned town, and they didn't become friends until he was almost out of high school. It would've been a less lonely life with KJ at her side.

"How are we on the finding his mom front?" he asked. "Has anybody seen her?"

Frankie sighed. "If they have, nobody's telling us."

"We have to find her," Ivy said. "I don't—I really don't know what else we can do."

Her grip on Frankie's hand was tight. Holding on for her life.

chapter eight

"So what's the deal with his mom?" KJ asked.

Frankie groaned. Then she snapped her mouth shut, glancing around to check for curious eyes. But it was 1 a.m. on a Monday, and Main Street was deserted.

"What do you mean what's her deal? You knew her." Frankie turned back to the poster she was pasting onto the door of Miss Petty's dress shop. There were no streetlights, and the clouds were dark over the thin moon. She could barely see Karin Martin's face beaming out at her from the poster.

KJ shrugged, smoothing thick paper over the wall before moving onto the next store. "I knew she was terrible. Fake polite all the way down, wouldn't piss on you if you were on fire. *Everyone should help themselves, make their own way,*" he crooned, in a decent approximation of the faint British accent she'd picked up during a vacation in her twenties and never let go.

"Nice."

"Thank you." KJ coughed, smearing his elbow over the paper until it stuck. "Anyway. I didn't know she was *this* bad. So your son dies and your husband runs off to Peru with the housekeeper. So what? Get a new husband. Get a stepkid. Don't call on your hometown's dark forces and get your dead son to possess his ex-girlfriend."

Frankie couldn't think of anything to say to that. It did sound pretty bad, losing your son and your husband within a couple of years.

"Honestly," KJ continued, slapping another poster onto the next wall. "I'm surprised she even bothered. I always got the feeling she didn't like him that much."

Frankie frowned. "What? Marvin was, like, his parents' pride and joy. Their legacy. The ultimate symbol of everything they'd accomplished—"

"Yeah, yeah. But I don't think they *liked* him. His mom definitely didn't. I had some classes with the guy. He was so, so freaked out to do anything she might disapprove of. Didn't Ivy tell you?"

"She said the family dinners were tense."

"I bet."

They came to a stop in front of the bakery. Frankie had to be back here in six hours. The very idea of it exhausted her. She set down the knapsack of posters they'd had to go three towns over to get printed and stretched her aching arms over her head.

"Glue," she instructed.

KJ held up the pot. Frankie slapped the brush over the bakery windows. KJ followed with the posters.

"Haven't seen that homeless guy," he said as they reached the last available spot on the window. "Maybe he left town. Was he even in on it?"

"I *thought* he was her lackey." Frankie brushed glue over a curling side of paper. It sagged under the weight of the glue. "Maybe I'm just paranoid."

"Wouldn't that be great?" KJ grinned, teeth glinting in the weak moonlight. "You're just being paranoid. Nightmares are just nightmares. That menacing stranger was just some guy passing through. Ivy isn't actually possessed, she just has a weird parasite that turns her eyes black, and Mrs. Martin isn't even back in town, it's another woman with a lion charm bracelet."

"Lion charms. Dime a dozen," Frankie murmured. "Crazy coincidence."

"Graduation goes off without a hitch," KJ continued. "We all go to New York and never come back here again."

"Happily ever after."

"Exactly."

They smoothed the final poster onto a store window and stood back to admire their work. The clouds drifted away from the sliver of moon, which shone enough to illuminate the words printed under Karin's picture-perfect smile:

HAVE YOU SEEN THIS BITCH?

The ride home was mostly silent. Frankie rested her head on the window and tried to picture skyscrapers, their impossible height. She'd never seen one in real life.

KJ turned down her street. "You tried getting out of town, right?"

Frankie frowned. "What? Of course."

"Wow. Thanks for telling me."

"You're coming to New York anyway. We weren't *ditching* you." Frankie yawned, jaw cracking around it. Sleep was so close she could feel it in front of her, heavy and deep and waiting for her to sink into it.

The car lights illuminated a pothole that had been embedded in this street since before she was born. KJ pulled over in front of Ivy's house and killed the engine. "If things get freaky, I'm out."

Frankie's hand paused on the door handle. Ivy's house lay in wait, a dark shape down the driveway. For a moment Frankie thought she'd slipped into a dream.

"Seriously," KJ continued. He fumbled in his pocket and brought out a pack of cigarettes. "I'll do posters, I'll read whatever book you throw at me. But if the gym starts burning down again and you're in it—I'm not coming to get you."

"*You* burned down the gym, man." Frankie felt her mouth tug up, automatic. But KJ's face stayed grave, hands tapping anxiously on the steering wheel. He wouldn't look at her.

Frankie snorted. "You set the embodiment of our evil town on fire for us, and stay *in* that evil town a year overdue so you can hang out, but you'll bail if things get scary? Sure."

"I *will*," KJ insisted. He bit down on a cigarette, mouth stretching in a sad facsimile of his usual careless grin. "I can't afford any more scars, next time might mess up my pretty face. The Molotov was a fluke, okay? I'm still a coward."

"You're not—"

"Yeah, yeah. Shut up." KJ's hands trembled around his lighter as he lit up, sucking in smoke like it would save his life. In the dark car, watching him smoke, Frankie couldn't help but remember him standing outside the school gym at Homecoming, his face overcast as he confessed he'd kissed a boy. The deep fear in his voice, the shaky hope. It was all fear now, fear and guilt and some dull deadness Frankie only heard once before, last year when he'd called her after a nightmare.

Smoke wafted up to the roof of the car. KJ sighed out a mouthful of gray.

"When it comes down to it, I'm still the same guy that set Dude up to get killed that day. With Hunter," he clarified when Frankie gave him a confused look. "And the gasoline. You heard about that, right?"

Frankie had a distant memory of it. She'd assumed it was another rumor.

"What happened?"

KJ shook his head. "It…Hunter told me to tell him where he could get Dude alone. I told him. He—cornered him. Doused Dude with gasoline and tried to light him up."

"Jesus."

"Yeah." KJ laughed, brief and mirthless. "I didn't even warn the guy. I knew what Hunter was capable of, and I just—led him right to him. We weren't going out, or anything. But Dude was a good guy. *Is* a good guy. He didn't deserve…"

He trailed off, taking another desperate drag. He'd been smoking less since last year, but sometimes Frankie caught him breathing it down with the determination of an alcoholic gulping a glass of whiskey.

Frankie thought about touching his knee. Decided against it. "He got away."

KJ made a self-deprecating noise in his throat. "Sure. No thanks to me."

Frankie stole his cigarette.

"Hey," he said, annoyed. He flexed his newly empty fingers at her. "Come on."

Frankie took a drag, relishing the murky taste. She'd all but given up since last year, when Ivy confessed she didn't like kissing smokers.

"You'll have our backs," she said, and blew a plume right at his eyes.

KJ waved it away. His hand was still shaking, but less so. Some of the dull deadness had drained out of his face.

"Hey." Frankie knuckled his shoulder until he looked at her again. "You will. I know it."

He smiled again, like he was humoring her, and reached for another cigarette.

"Come on, Frankie. Not everybody is as brave as you."

chapter nine

Lissiter stood outside the bakery in his cop gear. Head cocked, rubbing his temples. It was too hot for a hat.

Frankie was glad she'd applied deodorant before she left Ivy's house this morning. Her armpits were already damp. Karin Martin's face beamed out from every store window. Her beady eyes seemed to follow Frankie's every step.

Look innocent, she told herself. This wasn't a natural state for her. She'd spent most of her teenage years trying to look shifty, off-putting, dangerous. *Come near me if you dare.* Honestly, it was getting old. She was tired of the glares.

"Good to see you," Frankie called as she approached. "People have been complaining. Missing your donuts."

Lissiter did that jerking motion he often did when he looked at her, realized who he was looking at, and tried to pretend he didn't see her. It was less effective when she was walking right up to him.

"Not here to bake," he said, stepping out of the way to let her at the door. "You see this?"

Frankie gave a performative look up and down Main Street. "The posters? Yeah, weird. Is it all over town?"

"We don't know yet."

"Weird," Frankie repeated. Her key scraped against the lock. It was a difficult lock, you had to lean against the door a certain way for it to click open. She shoved her hip into the wood and jiggled the key hopefully. "No contact number? Posters usually have a contact number. You know, if someone sees that bitch."

"No number."

"Huh," Frankie said. "Weird."

Stop saying weird, Frankie thought in an exasperated voice that sounded a lot like Ivy's. She twisted the key, leaning harder against the door. It stayed stubbornly closed.

Lissiter cleared his throat. Frankie turned to find him staring past her at the posters, hand outstretched for...the keys?

Frankie held them out. Lissiter nodded curtly and stepped forward, ramming the door with one big shoulder and twisting the key in the lock.

The door sprung open.

"I'm usually better at that," Frankie said. "Um, thanks."

She held her hand out. Lissiter dropped the keys into them. He didn't want to touch her, Frankie supposed.

Mrs. Martin knocked me out and took my blood, Frankie imagined telling him. *She did the same to Ivy. Don't know what the hell she did with my blood, but Ivy's in a bad way. Spasms, screaming, trying to kill me. Mrs. Martin's poisoning the love of my life, Chief. What are you gonna do about it?*

Lissiter nodded at the posters. "We'll get these down later today."

"Thanks," Frankie repeated. She wanted to say more, maybe joke about the donuts—people really were annoyed by the lack of Lissiter food for sale—but she was sick of talking to people who couldn't meet her eyes.

What rumors did he believe? He thought she was dangerous, obviously, but how much? Did he buy into the dark magic or just the secret homosexuality? Was she a murderer in his eyes, cold-blooded and vicious?

Maybe he didn't know what he believed. Maybe he just knew that bad things happened around Frankie Tanner, and it was best to keep your distance.

Frankie gave him a two-fingered salute, walked into the bakery, and shut the door. It was strangely dark. She flipped on the light switch and frowned. Still dark.

The posters, Frankie realized. The posters blocked the windows, turning the bakery into a dim room silhouetted by Karin Martin's beaming face.

After work, Frankie went home.

Home-home. The place she put down on official forms. It was a pit stop, as so many of her visits home were. Pick up some things, drop some off, and head over to Ivy's. Even before April died, this was the kind of home you run from: stifling. Cold. Silent—except when it wasn't, and then you wished like hell it was quiet again.

But it had been quiet for years now. Frankie's sister was dead, her dad was gone, and her mom was either at work, at a bar, or asleep. It was like living with a ghost who occasionally remembered to do the grocery shopping. Frankie was so unused to seeing anyone else around that when she caught movement on the other side of the kitchen, she yelped.

"*Jesus*," spat Mary, her mom. "Holy hell, what is wrong with you?"

Frankie shoved the fridge shut. "What's wrong with you? Don't sneak up on me like that!"

"Not sneaking." Mary rubbed her chest. She'd jumped, actually jumped, at Frankie's shriek. "Gonna finish that?" She pointed at the orange juice Frankie was holding. Frankie took another sip, then handed it over. "Thanks." Mary wiped the rim and slugged the last few mouthfuls.

Frankie leaned back against the fridge and considered her. Hair washed, clothes clean. Her skin was clear of acne, which meant she'd been eating okay for a while, which meant she was brushing her teeth and doing better at work and drinking less.

Probably. Frankie had given up on interpreting her mother when she was a kid. No expectations meant you couldn't be disappointed. She yawned, rubbing her eyes. She was so damn *tired*.

Mary resurfaced from the juice carton. "So what are you doing in New York? Job lined up yet?"

Frankie couldn't remember the last conversation they'd had about New York. "Um. KJ's almost-roommate knows a cafe which has low standards and needs waitresses. And KJ's letting us sleep in his car until we find a place."

Mary nodded.

"Ivy's taking a pottery class," Frankie continued. She tried to keep going, but her voice splintered in her throat. Her tongue was thick and her vision was blurry. Frankie panicked for a terrified second, imagining thorns and vines and Marvin before feeling something wet coarse down her face and realizing: *oh shit, I'm crying.*

"Christ," Mary said. "Oh, shit, honey."

Frankie choked, sliding down the fridge onto the floor. She buried her head in her hands, cheeks red with tears and mortification. She hadn't cried in front of her mom since grade school.

"Sorry," she sobbed. "I don't know what this is."

"It's fine. It's…" Mary bent down, like she was soothing a wild animal with its leg caught in a bear trap. "You're okay."

"I'm so scared."

"Adulthood is scary."

Frankie laughed wetly. She'd never told her parents any of it—Babylove, rituals, creatures. The ruined soul of Bulldeen in a windy basement. April in her dreams, April crawling toward them with burning skin. Marvin and his cracked-open skull, jerking on the linoleum.

"Uh." Mary crossed her arms tight over her chest. Tanners were not born comforters. Everything Frankie learned about it, she learned from April, prickly and reluctant. Comforting Ivy was a constant learning process.

Mary cleared her throat. "I heard Ivy was sick?"

What else have you heard? We never talked about Homecoming, Mom.

"We don't know what's happening," Frankie croaked. "She's tired and she has, um, fits."

"Fits. Like…seizures?"

Frankie shrugged.

Mary squeezed her own elbows. She looked like she'd rather clean cat litter than be in this conversation, but she didn't leave. "Is it ongoing? Can you be a waitress if you have seizures? Won't you drop the tray?"

"I don't know." Frankie scrubbed at her face, eyeliner smudging over her palms. "Mom, I—"

Later, she would wonder what she was going to say. *Mom, I love her? Mom, I'm in over my head, I need help? Mom, I tried to get Ivy out of this cancerous town and she started dying so now we have to stay here until the thing that has us in its teeth stops goddamn chewing—*

A bang on the door.

"Jesus," they said in unison.

Mary lurched up, wincing over her bad knees. "Was that the door or did we get shot at? Christ in Heaven. Who the hell..."

She slouched out of the kitchen, still muttering. Frankie wiped her smudgy hands on her jeans and tried to steady her breathing. She'd have to tidy up her makeup before she left. Couldn't have all of Bulldeen seeing her like this. Maybe she could skip it and talk her mom into driving her over.

The front door opened. Mary's muttering cut off in a gasp.

Cold dread wormed into Frankie's gut. "Mom?"

Silence. Frankie staggered to her feet. "Mom? Who is it?"

"Nothing," came the thin reply. "I mean...it's fine."

Frankie's heart thudded into her throat, like she might throw it up right there in the kitchen. She rushed around the corner to find her mom staring, appalled and unmoving, at the front steps.

"Wait," she said as Frankie approached. "Don't—"

Frankie pushed her aside.

The dead cat lay stiff on the steps. It was brown and striped and scrawny. Blood leaked sluggishly down the wood from a small wound in its neck. No bite wound. Was this

58

Mrs. Martin, or just some frustrated Bulldeen neighbor wanting to ruin her night?

"I'll get a, uh…" Mary thumbed over her shoulder. The words took a while to make it to her mouth. "Bucket. Wait, a bag."

Frankie stopped her. "Has this happened before?"

"What? No." She rubbed her face, those sharp Tanner cheekbones. Frankie believed her, but there was something under her dazed disgust that she wasn't letting through.

Mary came back with a plastic bag and a cloth. Frankie held the bag open, and Mary lifted the rigid corpse into the bag by its back feet.

"Who the hell," Mary muttered as she dropped it in. "Poor damn *cat*."

Frankie tied the bag in a double knot. They'd been talking about pets, her and Ivy. Cats were easier for a landlord to agree to than dogs. Frankie would have to tell her they couldn't get one after all. She couldn't sit there with a cat on her lap without thinking of all the cats they'd buried.

Mary held her hand out. "I'll take it to the trash. You…start scrubbing."

Frankie hesitated. "This happened just before Homecoming."

"What?"

Frankie nodded at the plastic bag hanging between them.

Mary closed her eyes. "Shit. Really?"

"Really."

"Shit." Mary jerked the bag to her side, cheek twisting like she was biting it. "Why didn't you tell me?"

Frankie didn't bother gracing that with a response. She pointed down at the discolored stain they were standing in. "That's what this is from."

Mary jerked like she was going to step out of it. Then she sagged, as if taking that one step would be too much effort. Not for the first time, Frankie noticed how damn old she was getting. No one aged gracefully in Bulldeen.

Mary rubbed once more at her sharp cheekbones. Frankie waited for a sigh, a hiss, *this town is full of good for nothing shitheels*. More of the same. For somebody who lived here her whole life, she hated this town almost as much as Frankie did. Some of the best bonding they ever had was Frankie's mom gathering her up in her arms and saying, *don't listen to them, hon. They're a bunch of assholes.* Ironically, this was before the *real* bullying had started in high school. By freshman year her mom had all but checked out of her life, just like her dad. Just like April.

But Mary didn't hiss. Didn't sigh. She didn't speak for so long Frankie was about to get down and start scrubbing. But just as she was bending down to clear the stray blood spots from the wood, Mary spoke up.

"Ivy's sickness. Is it…" Mary clenched her eyes shut. "It's not—is it? Is…"

She was fumbling. The kind of fumbling you do when you don't know what question you're asking. The kind of question nobody asked in Bulldeen, just thought about in snatched moments before penning it away at the back of their brain.

"How much do you know?"

Mary shook her head. "People don't tell me things. But I still hear 'em. *Whispers.* 'Spect you know what that's like."

"I do." Frankie sucked in a breath. "It's not, um. Natural. Ivy's sickness."

"Can you stop it?"

"We're trying."

"Good. That's good." Mary's cheek kept denting inwards, chewing the tender skin. She looked like she'd take a thousand teary conversations on the kitchen floor over what she was about to say.

"I heard—April. At the dance you went to. I heard—" She stopped, a ragged noise clogging her throat. "Do I wanna know what happened?"

Frankie's ears were ringing at her sister's name. She hadn't heard either of her parents say it in months. She shrugged.

Mary snorted. "Oh, come *on*."

"I don't know," Frankie managed. "I don't think so."

Mary's mouth twisted. "Is she dead?"

"She's dead."

"Was she dead the whole time?"

"Yeah. Mostly. For a few weeks, she…" Frankie's dry lips moved wordlessly. How the hell could she sum up her averted resurrection attempt, all those guilt-ridden weeks of nightmares and dead cats culminating in April appearing in front of a gym full of dancers? *It's the kindness that kills you.* A line learned from their mom, a line Frankie had brought up while stabbing the creature wearing her undead sister back to death.

She couldn't say it. Frankie wet her lips. "But that's over. She's dead."

"Oh. O…kay." Mary nodded, eyes glassy. No surprise, no disappointment, no relief. Frankie couldn't tell what her mom was feeling, other than dazed. Then Mary's cheek pulled inward so hard Frankie could see the outline of her teeth, and a tear slipped down her cheek.

Frankie looked away. Mary did the same, as she had done in the kitchen, the two of them desperately trying to offer comfort without meeting each other's eyes.

"Okay," Mary repeated, and swiped the tear away. She looked down at the bag, the new bloodstains on top of the old, faded ones. Something gleamed in her eyes behind the grief and dull shock.

It was horror. Deep and dangerous and only starting to sink in. There was nothing like learning you've been living in the lion's mouth your whole life, waiting to be swallowed. Mary stared out at the neighborhood, empty rotting houses or full ones with people who could be relied on to leave a dead cat on their porch.

"Hon," Mary said. "You need to get the hell out of here."

"Mom," Frankie said. "I am *working* on it."

chapter ten

The bed was empty.

Frankie frowned, groping groggily at the mattress. It took an embarrassing amount of time to realize why Ivy being out of bed made her feel like her stomach was climbing up her throat.

Black eyes. Marvin. Marvin's jackass mom. Heart giving out over town limits. Those creepy black veins over Ivy's cheeks, taking root—

Frankie bolted to her feet. Okay. Calm. It was five-thirty in the morning. Ivy was probably in the bathroom. Or getting a glass of water. Or—

Frankie looked down at the bedframe. The ziptie they'd been using to chain her to the bedpost at night had been snapped, a broken circle. She touched the ragged pieces. Did Marvin-Ivy chew it off? Frankie would've felt a sudden movement. Her gaze fell on their stacked dinner plates on the nightstand. One of the steak knives stuck out from the pillow.

"Goddamnit," Frankie whispered. At least Martin hadn't killed her. That would've sucked. Wait—

She ran as quietly as she could to Ivy's parents' bedroom and peeked in. They breathed in tandem under the covers, curled together in the middle of the bed. It was sweet, even amid Frankie's growing panic.

Frankie headed back to Ivy's empty bedroom. She'd go searching, she decided as she pulled on the first shirt she could find. If that didn't work, she'd tell Ivy's parents. Talk them out of calling the cops. She could already imagine their panicked voices: *why didn't you wake us up as soon as you noticed she was gone?* What could Frankie even say to that? *Sorry, you seemed really stubborn on not accepting the whole black magic thing and I wanted to sort this out without holding your goddamn hands as you hyperventilate?*

Frankie pulled on her shoes and hesitated, bending to grab her leather jacket off the floor. It was too warm for a jacket, even this early in the morning. But there, in the right pocket: the comforting lump of her pocketknife.

Just in case.

No streetlights. No houses with their windows glowing. Just the moon and the faintest suggestion of sunrise. Had Frankie ever been outside this early? She must've, but she couldn't remember.

She ran the first two streets, swearing and whisper-yelling. Hoping like hell nobody saw her skulking around before dawn in sneakers and PJ bottoms and Ivy's old shirt from gym class. *Nefarious schemes*, they'd say. *What is Loser Tanner up to now?* No, they'd probably call her something other than Loser Tanner. They'd come up with worse nicknames in the past couple of years. Frankie didn't like to think of them.

On the third street, Frankie stopped. A familiar figure shuffled over a pothole at the other end of the street.

"*Ivy*," Frankie hissed, and then bit her lip. Maybe it would be better if she snuck up on her. Him? She didn't know if this was Ivy or Marvin or Bulldeen itself, that dark creature that had possessed April at Homecoming. Hateful, rotting thing. She still didn't know how much of this was Marvin and how much of it was Bulldeen, or if the two had melted into each other so much it no longer mattered.

Frankie crept closer, heart thudding hard. Her throat ached with phantom pain. She really didn't want to get strangled again. At least the steak knife was still accounted for, and Ivy's hands looked empty as they hung limp at her sides. The closer Frankie got the more Ivy looked…absent. Slack. Slumping and slow. Like she was sleepwalking. Her feet were bare, the cuffs of her PJ bottoms dragging on the asphalt.

Frankie braced herself. "Ivy?"

Ivy's plodding step didn't stutter.

Frankie touched her shoulder. "Sugarsnap?"

Nothing.

Frankie darted in front of Ivy. Ivy's eyes were...cloudy. Not black, but not normal either. Smoky gray, wisps of white gleaming through. Every few seconds there was a flicker of blue. Sky blue, cornflower blue. *I'd drown in that blue,* Frankie said once, hushed, into Ivy's neck. *I'd go happily. Drown me, baby.*

"Ivy." Frankie shook her gently. "Hey. Wakey-wakey. It's graduation day. We can't drag you over the stage when you're all creepy and white-eyed."

Ivy's head lolled.

Frankie wet her lips. *Bring her back to herself.* Right.

She cleared her throat. "Okay. So our first apartment in New York, we're going to have herbs in the window. And we *will* have windows, we're not getting a basement apartment just because it's cheaper. And we'll hang dried flowers from the ceilings, like you saw in that magazine. Lavender and roses. How's that?"

Ivy's eyes twitched, white and then gray under their half-closed lids. No blue.

Frankie sighed. New York talk worked to fend off Ivy's headaches, and sometimes when her nose started bleeding. Apparently this required sterner stuff.

"Hey—" Frankie froze.

Ivy's hands were at Frankie's throat. Not pressing—not yet. They were just resting, the pressure mounting and then stopping. Like something was holding her back.

Frankie swallowed. Her skin rode against Ivy's thumbs, pressed against the hollow of her throat.

"Okay. Okay, this is okay." She reached slowly into her jacket, hand closing around her knife. She was already sweating, stomach churning, but she made herself smile anyway.

"Remember our dance? Not ideal, with the fire and smoke and—and everything." She'd almost said *the dead*

65

body. Marvin probably wouldn't appreciate the reminder. "But it was romantic. Right? In that classic, big emotion, Jane Eyre way. Wait, Wuthering Heights. Which one had the burning down house? Anyway, it was super romantic. You and me under that disco ball as the music burned out. Remember, Ivy?"

Ivy's fingers twitched. Frankie held herself still as she could, hand shaking around the knife still hidden in her pocket.

"We didn't go to the next Homecoming," Frankie croaked. "We just—we dressed up and hung out in your room. We got that fancy popcorn from Little Hollow. We ate it on your bed and we slow-danced on your carpet."

Ivy's grip tightened. Not cutting off Frankie's breathing yet. Her eyes flickered—white, gray, blue. Her sleep shirt slid down her shoulder, revealing her sharp collarbone. She'd lost weight in the past few weeks. When she felt well enough to get dressed, she had to wear a belt so her skirt wouldn't fall off her hips.

"We did each other's hair," Frankie whispered. "You said I was the most beautiful thing you'd ever seen. Remember? Ivy?"

Ivy's lip curled. Her eyelids shuddered—white, gray, blue, white, gray, *black.*

Frankie pulled her pocketknife out of her jacket. The blade glinted in the moonlight. She'd stab her in the shoulder, the leg, somewhere shallow and non-fatal.

"Please don't make me do this," Frankie said.

Ivy's eyes swirled. Black, gray, black. Tendrils crept onto her cheeks. Ivy's grip *tightened*—

"Shit," Frankie choked, and lurched forward.

Ivy's mouth was cold. Her lips were slack. It felt strange, kissing someone who wasn't kissing back. Even when Frankie was kissing her awake, those lips would smile, kiss back, mumble something about coffee.

66

The pressure on her neck didn't stop. At first Frankie thought she'd screwed up. True love's kiss wouldn't bring the princess back, why did she ever think it could? Her pocketknife quivered in her sweaty hand. Tears welling in the corners of her eyes.

Sorry, Frankie thought, and brought the knife up.

The hands around Frankie's throat faltered. Frankie gasped, half-surprised and half with the relief of air down her windpipe. She kissed Ivy harder, breathing through her nose. *Come on. Come on—*

Ivy stumbled back. She wobbled, pitching sideways.

Frankie caught her elbows. "Ivy? Ives!"

Ivy blinked woozily, eyes tracking. "*Getthefuckout*," she mumbled, and winced. "Ow. *God*. Frankie?"

"Hi! You didn't try to kill me!"

Ivy squinted at her. Then at her neck, which Frankie was rubbing hard, still gulping air.

"I mean, at the end," Frankie allowed. "But you had a whole-ass knife earlier and you didn't stab me with it!"

"Whuh…" Ivy said, staring at the dark street around them. "Why are we in the road? What time is it? Why…"

She trailed off, gaze falling back on Frankie's neck. Frankie didn't know if she would bruise this time—whatever was in control of Ivy didn't squeeze very hard, not until the very end.

"You went walking," Frankie said. "Marvin didn't have the reins. Not all of them. You were fighting back."

Blood dripped from Ivy's nose. She wiped at it before Frankie could get to it.

"I'm a scrapper," Ivy said, still with the sluggish tongue of someone half-awake. She rubbed at her eyes, looking annoyed to find herself in her pajamas. "Was he…trying to get to his mom?"

"I guess? I don't know where else he has to go."

Ivy nodded. Her mouth wobbled, but quickly smoothed out. This was just another episode of their personal horror

67

show. Ivy had been getting more and more resigned. Less scared. She'd spit something in Marvin's voice and when she came back to herself she'd just...nod. Like this was business as usual. A sickness she had to put up with.

Ivy sighed. "What time is it?"

"Almost dawn. Oh, hey." Frankie pointed at the first blush of sunrise.

Ivy turned to watch it. Frankie had never seen anyone so exhausted. Even Ivy's blinks came slowly.

The sun kept bleeding into the sky. The silence grew. The red sunrise climbed Ivy's flyaway hair, her hollow cheek. In any other circumstance, Frankie would think it was romantic. A strange feeling was overtaking her, almost déjà vu but not quite. The sensation that they'd never be here again.

She took Ivy's hand. After a moment, Ivy's fingers curled around hers.

"Frankie?"

"Yeah?"

"If I try to hurt you again, you have to kill me. You know that, right?"

Frankie didn't answer. She squeezed Ivy's hand—strangely cold despite the warm morning—and the two of them watched the last Bulldeen sunrise they'd ever see.

chapter eleven

Nobody dared to make eye contact with Ivy as they paid for their pastries. They would glance behind the counter to see who was sitting beside the trashcan, then their gazes would snap anywhere else. Their muffin, their wallet, the torn linoleum.

It was a strange sight, Frankie supposed: a former cheerleader in sweatpants and a borrowed black shirt, hunched miserably on the floor behind the bakery counter. Something Bulldeen locals would look away from even if it wasn't Ivy Wexler, half of a dark magic duo.

"Have a great day," Frankie told the customers every time they pretended not to see.

Without fail, the customers would shoot her a wary look before fleeing. It freaked them out even more when she was polite.

When the bell over the door chimed again near lunch, she was ready with a razor smile.

"He-*llo*, welcome to…" She trailed off.

Lissiter blinked, hands flexing around a cardboard box. Frankie wished he was wearing the apron. He was less intimidating in an apron. When he wore that tatty green thing, she could almost convince herself she liked him.

She shifted anxiously from foot to foot, hoping he'd do something to break the tension. Maybe make a joke. *You're dealing out greetings now? Did the boss give you a bonus for your last day?*

But Lissiter wasn't a jokey guy. At least, not with her.

"Delivery," he said, holding out the box as far as it would go so he didn't have to step closer. "Miss Petty. Picking it up at five."

Frankie took the box and rocked it lightly. "Doesn't sound like a carrot cake. Petty's branching out."

Lissiter's annoyance at the box shake gave way as he noticed Ivy sitting on the floor behind the counter, greasy hair slick against the trashcan.

"What's with her?"

Frankie shrugged. "Hangover. Got too excited celebrating graduation."

She smiled bitterly. *Go on,* she dared him as he shifted uneasily. *Call me out on the lie. Press the situation. Protect and serve us, motherfucker.*

His expression ticked from unease into genuinely disturbed. Frankie twisted to see Ivy wiping blood off her upper lip. The nosebleeds were coming and going. A pile of paper napkins lay next to Ivy's knee, half of them crimson and crumpled around her.

Her head twitched, a vein standing out in her neck. Frankie's hand shot into her pocket, curling around her knife, but Ivy's gaze stayed clear blue.

"You know how it is," Frankie told Lissiter. "Hey, good job getting the posters gone."

Lissiter paused, half-turned toward the door. "Storeowners did most of it. Still some up on the walls between stores. We'll get somebody on it."

"Any whispers about the bitch?"

Lissiter gave her a stern look.

Frankie grinned. "What? Just saying what the posters called her."

"Nobody's seen her."

"Shame." Frankie leaned over to the glass, sliding a finger over the marks of paper still stuck to the other side of the window. Whoever pulled them off didn't do a good job, with shards of pulp and glue sticking where the corners used to be.

"Well," Lissiter said stiffly. He nodded at the box on Frankie's counter. "That's that. Guess I better—"

Ivy's voice wavered up from the floor. "Do you still have Kate's number?"

Lissiter stopped. One foot in the doorway. For a moment Frankie thought he'd just keep walking, but apparently the question was confusing enough to make him turn.

"What?"

"Chief Higgins. Sorry—ex-chief," Ivy clarified, wobbling to her feet. She was wearing sneakers, the kind you can shove on without having to tie any laces. Anything else was too much effort.

He stared at her. Actually stared, not looking at her side-on, not glancing. No immediately looking away when she caught him at it, either.

A chill crept down Frankie's spine. Frankie couldn't remember the last time he hadn't looked away when she caught him staring. His brow was wrinkled, his mouth ajar. He was a man of few expressions, and Frankie had never seen this one.

Shock. Dismay. Vague…hurt? His gaze darted to Frankie like he was asking for confirmation, *did she really just ask me that,* and Frankie looked back at him expectantly. *Sure did, dude. What's the problem?*

"Or Milly Hart's," Ivy continued when Lissiter didn't reply. Her head twitched. Frankie's hand did the same in her pocket, sweating around her knife.

"We're having a problem," Ivy said through her teeth. "We think they could be able to help."

Lissiter's brow unwrinkled. Finally, he averted his gaze. "No."

"No to both?"

Lissiter clenched his belt. "No to both," he muttered. There was something underneath his words, something important, something that made Frankie feel as if she missed something crucial, but Lissiter was already leaving. Before the door could swing shut behind him, he reached out and caught it.

"Have a good graduation," he said, and left.

Ivy sank back to the floor amongst her pile of bloody napkins. A fresh line of red tracked down her chin.

Frankie knelt and wiped it off. "How are you feeling?"

"Like you should lock me in the walk-in."

Frankie laughed.

Ivy didn't. Sweat beaded on her forehead. "I think...you need..." she groped for Frankie's shoulders. No—her neck. Black flashed through her irises. *You need to bring me back.*

"The first note you ever gave me—I had it up in my locker until we left. It's in my suitcase now." Frankie kept her breathing even as Ivy's hands trembled on her collarbones. "I'll put it up in our apartment in New York. On a mirror, maybe. Somewhere we can look at it all the time and remember how we started. We'll have to come up with a story, by the way. We can't tell people you invited me over to sacrifice me for necromancy reasons and then I was just so darn cute you decided not to."

"Not what happened," Ivy croaked. Her hands peeled away from Frankie's neck.

"Kind of what happened, sugarsnap." Frankie brushed Ivy's damp hair back and smiled. Ivy smiled back shakily. She was still sweating, but there was no new blood from her nose and her eyes were clear again.

The bell rang over the door. Frankie shot up, sending the customer who'd just come in a tight smile that they steadfastly ignored.

Ivy reached up for her wrist. "Frankie. Seriously. Lock me in the walk-in."

"Sure. Here you go, Mr. and Mrs. Wexler, your daughter's a popsicle." Frankie handed her Miss Petty's box. "Go put this out back. And grab more napkins."

"And lock myself in the walk-in so I don't strangle anybody," Ivy muttered as she staggered off.

The customer, Mrs. Daily, didn't look up from examining the shelf of pastries. She stared at a croissant with an intensity that meant she'd heard every word and refused to acknowledge it.

Frankie leaned on the counter. "What can I get you today?"

Mrs. Daily cleared her throat. "The, uh...plum danish."

"Oooh. *Fancy* today." Frankie bagged the danish and handed it over. "Have a great day."

Mrs. Daily threw the money on the counter and fled. Frankie pocketed the extra fifty cents she'd left—out of panic, obviously; Mrs. Daily was *not* a tipper—and let out a long breath in the silent shop. Just a few more hours. Then they'd close early and head over to the graduation ceremony. Mr. and Mrs. Wexler were picking them up from the bakery, gowns in the backseat for them to put on during the ride over. They'd discussed having dinner after the ceremony at the only diner in town, but the talk petered out pretty quickly with one glance at Ivy in her bed, sweating and trembling and swearing in someone else's voice.

Frankie put her face in her hands and sighed. She was so goddamn exhausted. She wanted to sleep. She wanted a joint. She wanted to lie down in Ivy's arms and not have to worry about getting murdered.

"Ives," she called. "Remember to put the box on the right shelf. The left one still unhooks sometimes. Lissiter leaves pissed-off notes when his orders fall off and get smooshed."

No answer.

"Ivy?"

Nothing. Dread climbed Frankie's spine.

It's fine, she told herself as she walked, dead-legged, toward the kitchen. *She's just locked herself in the walk-in. Or a bunch of boxes fell on her and she's too busy shoving them back onto the right shelf to answer.*

The kitchen was empty. Frankie walked to the walk-in freezer, heart sinking as she heaved the door open.

Cold air drifted out. The scent of cheese and meat and rot.

No Ivy.

"Shit," Frankie said, and sprinted full pelt for the back door. It hung open, breeze bouncing it against the doorframe.

"Holy Jesus Christ shit crap god," Frankie said. It didn't feel like enough. She punched the door fully open and screamed into the dirty alleyway. No one came looking. No one ever looked in Bulldeen.

"Should've locked her in the walk-in," Frankie panted. "Should've—*goddamnit*."

What now? Call Ivy's parents? Walk out of the job right now and roam the streets shouting Ivy's name? Start grabbing people and scream *someone's gotta know where Marvin's mom is, say something, you sons of bitches, I'm not leaving until I have her crushed windpipe under my hands*—

A distant bell. Someone was coming in the front door.

Frankie spared one more scream and then charged back into the front of the store.

"We're closed," she snapped. "Get—"

She stuttered to a stop.

The homeless man ducked his head, hood obscuring his eyes.

"Uh," he said. "Uh, I…Hello."

"Hello." Frankie swallowed. Something itched at the back of her head. The man had clean nails. Polished boots. Dirty face, beard peeking out from under his hood. Strange, lumpy nose, skin peeling where the nose blended into cheek.

"I was—I was just checking," he said, and turned to leave.

Frankie stalked out from behind the counter. "Who the hell are you? What's your name?"

"Uh. Rich…Richard." The man glanced back at the door.

Frankie leapt in front of it. "Richard what? Where are you from? Got any kids, Richard?"

"Richard…S-Summer," the man stammered. "From, uh. Uh. New York?"

"Kids?"

A beat. "No," the man said, and the weight behind the word was as much confirmation as Frankie needed.

She bared her teeth. "Where the FUCK is Ivy?"

"What? I don't...Ivy..." the man blustered, looking past her desperately.

Frankie checked behind her. Nothing through the windows but an empty Main Street. "What, looking for your *wife*? Or is she busy?"

"Look," said the man. "I think we should both take a step back and—"

Frankie shoved him. "You take her, you take me too."

Mr. Martin stumbled back. Frankie didn't remember his name. How could he be so involved in this and she didn't know his name? Maybe it really *was* Richard. Though he sure sounded like he was bullshitting.

He sighed. "I only just talked her out of that."

Then he lunged. He was twice her size. Frankie fumbled in her pocket for her knife, but it was too late: his big hands had her shoulders. He pushed, and that was all it took.

Frankie hit the ground headfirst. The world went black.

chapter twelve

Pain flared at the base of Frankie's skull. She groaned.

"Oh thank god," said Mr. Martin. "I thought I'd killed you."

"Isn't that the plan?" Frankie slurred, and opened her eyes. She was lying in the middle of a cavernous living room. A sheet lay over the table and couch, like they were waiting for movers. The curtains were drawn, dust collecting on the wooden floor.

"Where are we?" Frankie tried to sit up, but arms were tied behind her back, and she was quickly discovering she didn't have the core strength to sit up without them.

Mr. Martin sat on the sheeted couch on the other side of the room, twisting his hands together. His face was…different. Clean, and…was his *nose* like that before? It looked like Marvin's now, that snub nose she always loathed.

"You put on a fake nose," Frankie realized. "What is this, Scooby-Doo?"

"I'm sorry," he said. She couldn't tell if he was apologizing for the kidnapping or the stupidity of the fake nose.

Frankie couldn't laugh. The panic was setting in now, cold and terrible. Where were they? Where was Ivy? Where was Mrs. Martin, and what the hell were they going to do? Did anyone see her get taken from the bakery, and if so, did they give enough of a shit about her to alert somebody, or would they call it good riddance to bad rubbish?

She blinked hard, her eyes adjusting to the darkness. A circle of candles stood around her, unlit.

Frankie forced back tears. "What—what are you going to do to me?"

Mr. Martin's face twisted. Before he could say anything, a voice rang down the hall, honey-smooth.

"Is that her? Is she awake yet?"

Frankie whispered, "Don't tell her."

Mr. Martin paused. But not for long. "She's awake."

"Good. Come help me with the other one."

Frankie twisted toward the door Mr. Martin left through. *Other one* could only mean one thing, right? She waited, heart in her throat, but all she heard was scuffling, footsteps, a hissed argument she couldn't catch.

Frankie wiggled until she could feel her pocketknife in her jeans. *What kind of idiot doesn't take weapons off their kidnappee? If only I could reach the goddamn thing!* She looked around desperately. There was nothing nearby she could use to cut herself free, just wood and dust and candles. Were they in the old Martin house? It would make sense, it looked fancy and abandoned.

She pulled at her restraints. What had they tied her with? It felt rough and thin and...weak. Like if she just yanked enough—

Karin Martin emerged from the hallway, scowling, hair hidden in a beanie and figure obscured by her baggy clothes. She looked uncharacteristically scruffy, but at least she hadn't rubbed dirt into her face to impersonate a homeless guy.

"She can't be *that* heavy," she complained. "Come on. *Move.*"

Mr. Martin staggered through the door, Ivy slung over his shoulder. It was almost a relief to see her struggle against her restraints—it meant she was still Ivy.

"Hey," Frankie rasped as Mr. Marvin placed her girlfriend beside her in the candle circle. "You okay, sugarsnap?"

Ivy looked up at her, voice muffled by the gag in her mouth.

Karin scoffed. "Why isn't she gagged? And why aren't her legs tied? Honestly, I have to do everything around here—"

77

Mr. Martin caught her before she could move forward. "I—look. Karin. Let's think about this."

She gave him a disgusted look. "We've *talked* about it, Bob. Let's get this over with."

Frankie shuddered, inching closer to Ivy, curling their ankles together as best she could with Ivy's feet bound.

"Should've locked you in the walk-in," she whispered. "Sorry."

Ivy made a noise under her gag that might've been a laugh. Her cheeks were wet, her eyes bloodshot and shot through with black. Shudders wracked her frame.

"Hey. *Hey*." Frankie nosed at her forehead. "We're gonna be fine, alright? Just gotta…find a way out of these things. Then we'll go to graduation—shit, what time is it? Did we miss graduation?"

Ivy buried her face in Frankie's neck. Frankie couldn't help it—she flinched. But there was no bite, no Marvin weaseling his way through. Just Ivy, scared and sobbing and gagged, trying to steal a shard of comfort in her girlfriend's arms.

Frankie smeared a kiss against Ivy's forehead.

"We're okay," she promised "We're—"

"What are you waiting for? Go get the knife!" said Karin.

Frankie twisted on the floorboards. Mr. Martin slumped toward the door, Karin watching him go with her lips in a tight line. Though her eyes were heavy with bags, everything about her screamed determination. There was no talking her out of this. But maybe they could stall.

Frankie sucked in a shaky breath. "So what's the plan? Kill me, give the town power to secure Marvin a permanent spot in Ivy's body? That's not how it works."

Karin snorted. "Like you know how it works," she sneered, and for a moment she was a mirror image of the woman who gave her judging looks in the supermarket. "If you knew how it worked, you would've brought April back properly."

Frankie gestured at Ivy with her chin. "How is this PROPER! It's not even his body!"

"Yes. Well." Karin kneaded her temples. Her nails were gel, Frankie noted faintly. Half of them, anyway, the real nail starting halfway up and then ending in a fake purple claw.

"The town's weak," Karin continued. "Those—what did the kids call them, *Dead Freaks?* Took care of that. I had *hoped* we could do the same thing they did. Bring Marvin back in his own body, sacrifice some miscreants in return. But it's so weak, it told us—it gave us these *ridiculous* instructions, said it was the best it could do, and now—" She waved at Ivy curled up on the floor. "Now all we have is *this* thing, Marvin *and* the town's dirty soul bound up in Ivy damn *Wexler's* body. *I* still think it should have been you. We even took your blood, but *no*, Marvin said it had to be his damn ex-*girlfriend.*"

Frankie nodded, like she actually gave a shit, and yanked her arms against her restraints. They strained under the attention. If she pulled them enough they'd break, but did they have time? What else could she do? If they were at the abandoned Martin house, that meant the school field was across the road. Maybe graduation was happening right now, her mom and Ivy's parents sitting in those awful plastic chairs in the dry grass, wondering where their daughters were. If she screamed for help, maybe…no, they weren't *that* close.

"It will be an adjustment," Karin continued. "But he wants her. And why shouldn't he? She was a lovely girl, before you put that dark seed in her. Before you poisoned her. Now look at her."

Frankie laughed against Ivy's lank hair. "Pretty sure this is *your* doing, ma'am! You and your shitty husband. You know they're saying he ran off to Hawaii with your maid?"

"It was *Milwaukee*," Karin hissed. "And he came back once I told him the plan."

Slow footsteps. Frankie twisted to watch Mr. Martin come back into the room holding a steak knife. It looked strangely small in his big hand, which trembled as he handed the knife over.

"*There.* Was that hard?" Karin tapped the knife against her thigh, hyping herself up. "Well, then. Let's—let's do this."

Ivy sobbed behind her gag. Her eyes flickered, blue, black, blue…

"We're okay," Frankie told her, voice breaking. "Shit. Ives, we're okay—"

"What are you waiting for," Karin snapped at her husband. "Don't just stand there, *help* me!"

Mr. Martin stumbled toward the circle. Ivy struggled up and threw herself over Frankie with a strangled noise that only intensified as Mr. Martin dragged her off.

"We're okay," Frankie croaked senselessly. "Ivy, look at me, we're alright."

Mr. Martin held her by her shoulders. "I'm sorry," he said as his wife approached, knife in hand. "I'm so sorry."

"If you're so sorry then *help* us," Frankie snapped, and dragged in a quivering breath. "HELP! HOLY SHIT, SOMEBODY HELP US—"

Mr. Martin covered her mouth. Frankie cried out against it, terrified. The last time she'd been this scared was when Not-April was on top of Ivy, biting chunks out of her arm while Ivy shrieked in agony.

Karin bent down in front of her, knife up. "Keep her steady."

Mr. Martin panted. "Candles."

"What? Oh, damnit." Karin dug in her pocket. "Did you have the lighter?"

Frankie twisted her arms behind her as they argued over who had it last. It felt like rope. Shitty, dry, *thin* rope that would snap if she just yanked long and hard enough. Now she just needed time.

Karin drew a lighter out of her husband's pocket with an infuriated sigh and started lighting the candles.

"We can figure this out," Frankie pleaded. "We can find someone else. We can sacrifice other people. There's gotta be someone you want dead more than me."

Karin's head whipped up, flame hovering above the last candle. She gave Frankie such a scathing look Frankie shrank back against Mr. Martin.

"Alright," Frankie said. "Dumb thing to say. Got it."

Karin lit the last candle and stood, still with that hateful look on her face. Frankie couldn't look at it, turning instead to Ivy, who was writhing across the floorboards in small, stubborn increments. Trying to get to Frankie.

"Keep her still," Karin instructed her husband. She started to chant under her breath. *"Bulldeen, I invoke thee. Come and feed."*

Wind picked up in the dark room. Dust blew into everyone's eyes.

"Wait," Frankie said, kicking out desperately. "Wait, wait, *wait*—"

Karin shoved her legs away and raised the knife. Frankie screamed.

Ivy's voice drowned them both out. "I KILLED HIM," she shouted, trembling with the effort of keeping her voice her own. She bared her teeth at Karin. She'd used a raised nail on the floorboards to yank her gag out. "And it wasn't an accident. I hated him so much. I'm glad he's dead. Your son was *poison*."

That's one way to buy time. Frankie forced down a hysterical laugh as she strained her arms against her restraints. She could feel them creak.

Karin made a wounded noise. Her lower lip trembled. "Marvin, are you sure you don't want her? I really—I'd *love* to kill this bitch."

Blood dripped from Ivy's nose. Her eyes flickered. Black, blue, black, *black.*

81

"*N-no*," said Marvin, using Ivy's throat. "*I…want…her. I want…to do it. It says…more. Power.*"

"Oh, for goodness sake." Karin dangled the knife in front of him. "If I give you this, you'll keep control of her until it's over? I don't want to hurt that body any more than we have to. There's wear and tear and there's a giant stab wound, hon."

Marvin-Ivy grinned. Black veins crept from his eyes into his cheeks. "*I…have…control.*"

"Much more convincing if you stopped *twitching*, hon." But Karin bent down obediently and sliced him free. First his arms, then his legs. Marvin-Ivy crouched on the floorboards like an animal before his head snapped up, glaring up at Frankie with delighted hatred.

Frankie shrank back against Mr. Martin, who actually took a step back.

"Careful," Karin snapped. "Keep her in the circle!"

"Sorry." Mr. Martin's big hands trembled around Frankie's shoulders.

Marvin-Ivy held out a spasming hand out to his mother.

"Careful," Karin repeated, softer, and handed him the knife.

Marvin nodded. His eyes were fully black now, focused entirely on Frankie. Frankie's skin crawled. *How much of it is him and how much of it is the town?* She had no idea. She never really knew what Marvin was capable of. But taking over his ex-girlfriend's body to kill Frankie—that sounded like him.

Marvin crawled over with the spasming movements that Frankie remembered from April, that fateful Homecoming dance. Two girls who loved Frankie very much fighting every move their puppet master made.

Frankie forced a laugh. "Hey, man. Remember when I punched you and you cried like a bitch?"

Marvin's smile twisted. "*I'll…enjoy…this.*"

"Remember when Ivy killed you?" Frankie pushed back further into Mr. Martin, pulling tight at her bonds. Almost. She was so close.

"Remember those teeth in your brain?" Frankie said shakily as Marvin-Ivy leaned over her. "Did you feel it, Marv? Did you hear that wet suck of April eating your *fucking* brain, you pathetic little shit?"

Marvin-Ivy growled. His eyes flickered, a hint of white shooting through. He raised the knife.

"*Stop...moving.*"

"You can't have her," Frankie said. "She's mine and I'm hers. We belong to each other, you aren't anywhere in that equation. Hear me, sugarsnap?"

"*Stop,*" Marvin-Ivy repeated. He gritted his teeth. His eyes flickered again—black, blue, *blue.* Sky blue, ocean blue, the blue of that skyline they were going to escape into.

I'd drown in that blue, Frankie had told her.

Frankie didn't want to die.

She yanked. The ropes snapped behind her. Frankie grabbed for her jeans pocket, and Marvin-Ivy's smile froze.

"*Don't,*" he hissed, and lurched forward.

Marvin-Ivy's knife sunk into her shoulder. Frankie's pocketknife skated along his elbow. Both of them screamed, Karin lunging to help, Mr. Martin stumbling back in shock and letting Frankie fall to the floor.

Karin's mouth fell open in a shriek. "GET—"

A car crashed through the living room wall.

83

chapter thirteen

Frankie's shoulder throbbed.

She couldn't see where the knives went, they'd gotten lost when half of the living room turned to splinters. Amid the rubble, the car's engine stuttered to silence where it had rear-ended the couch.

KJ climbed out of the driver's seat.

"Oh shit," he said faintly.

A hand locked around Frankie's wrist. Frankie screamed.

"It's okay," Ivy said, rushed. Her arm bled where Frankie had skimmed her with the pocketknife. Her eyes were blue and nothing else. Her grip was gentle, insistent, tugging Frankie out of the circle.

Mr. Martin sprawled against the wall behind them, groaning. He'd hit his head when the car crashed in.

Karin lay face down in the remains of the circle. The candles were snuffed, all except for one wobbling straggler by Karin's head. The lone flame swelled. Karin twitched.

"Oh shit," Frankie said, and crawled back faster. Where did her pocketknife go? She must've dropped it during the crash. Wait, where was the *other* knife—

Karin's hand shot out and grabbed Frankie's ankle, fingers closing in a jerky yet iron grip, tugging her back into the broken circle.

Ivy grabbed Frankie's wrists and pulled. "Let GO of her!"

A wet laugh rumbled from Marvin-Karin's throat. Black bled from her eyes onto her cheeks, burrowing in deep. Blood leaked from her nose into her grinning mouth.

"Dude," Frankie said, incredulous. "Your *mom*?"

Still clinging to Frankie, Ivy turned toward KJ. "What are you DOING?"

KJ stood next to the driver's seat, twisting the keys desperately in the ignition. "One second! The car won't start! We need a getaway vehicle!"

"KJ YOU SHITHEAD GET OVER HERE," Frankie screamed, aiming another kick at Marvin-Karin's head.

KJ twisted the keys again. The car spluttered pathetically in reply.

There. Lying in an ocean of splinters and the detached arm of the couch sat Frankie's pocketknife, splayed open and shining in the candlelight. Which, she noticed with a sinking dread, was growing. The wall next to Mr. Martin was on fire and the flames were climbing fast, acrid smoke rising to the ceiling.

Frankie pointed toward the detached couch arm, ignoring the throb of agony it sent up her injured shoulder. "KNIFE!"

Ivy looked past her at Marvin-Karin, who was clawing up Frankie's legs.

"*Stay,*" Marvin-Karin begged, voice hoarse, black veins bulging in its cheeks. The people had been crowded out. It was Bulldeen who pleaded.

"*You have to stay,*" it continued, gel nails digging into Frankie's knees. "*I can't—there's no food. The poison, it's almost run dry. I'll die if you don't let me feed.*"

"Then fucking DIE," Frankie shrieked, kicking the monster in the face. Marvin-Karin's nose cracked, blood turning from a drip to a torrent, spilling down its chin onto Frankie's jeans. Its grip stayed, a vice around Frankie's knees.

Ivy ran up behind her. Frankie reached out, but Ivy rushed past her. She stabbed Marvin-Karvin in the back.

The monster howled. Ivy brought the knife down again and again, a guttural cry wrenching out of her throat.

We've been here before, Frankie thought, and yelled, "It has to be her first! Or—him? I don't know, it has to be a person again before you do the heart-stab!"

"Well I can't make them themselves," Ivy yelled back, still stabbing. "I don't know what to say! I *hate* these goddamn people!"

A low groan made them turn. Mr. Martin swayed toward them, head in his hands. Flames scaled the wall behind him. The kitchen knife glinted in his grip, throwing firelight.

Ivy raised Frankie's pocketknife at him. Frankie gestured for her to wait.

"Please," Frankie tried. "Mr—um, Bob. Let us go. Stop your wife and your son and this soul-sucking goddamn *town* and…and let us go."

The knife shook at Mr. Martin's side. His face twisted as he watched his wife's body writhe, full of wounds and darkness. Beyond it, the final candle threw sparks.

"Please," Frankie begged. The smoke made her cough. "We just want to get out of here. Live our lives."

She moved in front of Ivy, reaching a hand back instinctively. Ivy held it. Ivy's hand was wet with blood, dusted with splinters, calloused from picking incessantly for weeks. Frankie clutched it like it was the rest of her life.

Mr. Martin blinked. Once, twice, three times, like he was absorbing the answer to a very important question. Frankie heard the car stall and KJ curse.

Mr. Martin turned to what was once his wife. "We promised we'd only do this if they were bad people."

"*What?*" Karin's voice scraped up her throat. "*We…never…said that!*"

"I thought…" Mr. Martin looked at Frankie helplessly.

"*Bob*," Marvin-Karin croaked. Then, in a slightly different voice: "*Dad.* You…can't…let them…do this."

Mr. Martin drew in a shuddering breath, his eyes full of tears. "No. I can't."

"Wait!" Frankie sat up and grabbed at Ivy, the two of them bracing for the inevitable attack. But Mr. Martin just bent down and helped pry Marvin-Karin's hands off

Frankie's legs. Frankie crawled back, Ivy's hands on her in an instant, dragging her up.

"You're okay," Ivy whispered, cupping Frankie's face. "You're okay, are you okay?"

Frankie kissed her bloody chin. "I'm—"

Karin's own voice spilled out of her throat, devastated. "Honey? What are you doing?" Then, in a rougher voice which Frankie couldn't tell if it was Marvin or monster, *What are you doing?*"

Mr. Martin bent close. "Just let them live their lives," he whispered, and plunged the knife into its heart.

The creature cried out. Behind it, the lone candle guttered.

Frankie squeezed Ivy's hands, her eyes watering with smoke. It was getting thicker now, the flames licking up the walls.

The body turned to ash. Mr. Martin whimpered.

The car was working again, rumbling like a sick animal. KJ slapped the car roof. "GET IN! GET THE HELL IN, JESUS CHRIST!"

Frankie and Ivy stumbled toward it.

Ivy winced. "Your shoulder—"

"Go," Frankie told her.

They climbed in the backseat. As Frankie yanked Ivy's seatbelt on, her gaze caught something beyond the windshield.

It was almost lost in the smoke. But for a second Frankie got a glimpse: Mr. Martin hacking into his elbow, wobbling to his feet next to a pile of ash that was once his wife's body. Frankie eyed it, waiting for a thornfruit to emerge and rot back into it, the way it had done with April.

The ash stayed still.

KJ stomped on the accelerator. They jerked backward. Frankie fell against the seat.

"Come on," Ivy said, leaning against her seatbelt to help her up.

The car careened back into the yard, carving a circle into the dirt as KJ turned around and drove out through the hole he'd made in the fence.

Frankie stared at the ruined fence. "What—"

"I was in a hurry, okay? Lissiter told me—oh, Jesus." KJ stared out at the old Martin house, billowing smoke. "I need to stop setting shit on fire."

Ivy let out a hitching laugh into Frankie's hair. Frankie pulled away and checked her over. Ivy's face was covered in blood and tears, the skin next to her mouth picked into an angry scab—but her eyes were blue. No black veins wormed into her cheeks.

KJ stopped in the middle of the street. "Where are we going? Hospital? Do we need to get your suitcases—"

"Go," Frankie croaked. "Let's get the hell out of here. I can't spend one more second in this town."

"Got it," KJ said. "Oh, shit. Company."

Frankie followed his gaze. The school field was across the street. Everyone was up from their plastic chairs, robed students flowing down from the stage. They were almost at the fence. Leading the charge was Mr. and Mrs. Wexler dressed in their best clothes, Frankie's mom hanging at their side in her cleanest pair of jeans. They gaped in horror at the burning house their children had just driven out of.

Ivy rolled the window down. "SEE YOU LATER! WE LOVE YOU!"

Frankie slapped KJ's seat. "Drive."

The car jolted into motion. Frankie twisted to watch Mr. and Mrs. Wexler start to run after the car before Frankie's mom stopped them. Frankie waved, shoulder throbbing with the motion. Her mom raised a hesitant hand back, then faded from sight.

The streets were empty. No one stopped them as they sped toward the town limits, wheels screeching, taking up both lanes to turn corners.

Ivy squeezed Frankie's hands hard enough to turn her knuckles white, eyes fixed on the battered WELCOME TO BULLDEEN sign coming up fast. Frankie drank in the sight of her, mildly healthy and probably whole, sweaty and pale and trembling but here, alive, *escaping—*

The welcome sign flew past. Frankie raised her middle finger at it.

KJ let out a triumphant yell. "Are we good? Is Ivy heart-attacking?"

"We're good," Ivy said, and the relief in her voice made Frankie want to cry. She tugged Ivy up to kiss her forehead, her nose, her scabbing lips. Ivy kissed back desperately, smiling against her mouth.

They were *out.* They were bleeding and crying and they had no spare clothes, toothbrushes, or anything else they had packed in the suitcases waiting at Ivy's house, but they were *out.* None of them turned back to watch the thickening black plume of smoke.

Ivy pulled back with a shaky laugh. "Did you—did you buckle me in, back there? You're the one who got *stabbed!*"

"And you're the one who got *possessed* for *weeks!*" Frankie cupped her face, so familiar and so lovely in her palms. "How do you feel?"

Ivy   beamed.   "Free."

chapter fourteen

The phone rang.

Frankie groaned. She was only half-conscious, buried in her favorite place in the world: bed. *Their* bed, in *their* tiny apartment, wrapped in *their* scratchy sheets. Technically the sheets belonged to the last person who lived here, who had ditched without paying three weeks of rent or taking half their stuff, but now it was theirs.

"Ivy," Frankie mumbled. "Phone."

Ivy pushed her icy feet into Frankie's shin.

"Jesus!" Frankie flailed, twisting around to wrap Ivy in her arms. "War criminal. We agreed on no cold feet fights."

Ivy made a sleepy noise against Frankie's collarbone and snuggled closer. Frankie smiled into the pillow. She couldn't get up *now*.

The phone rang out until the answering machine clicked on: "Hi, girls!"

Ivy made another noise into Frankie's chest. When it came to phone calls, there were three possibilities: one, KJ, who lived a few blocks over. Two, their boss calling to say someone was sick and could one of them please come down to the cafe to cover a shift? And three, Ivy's parents. More accurately it was Ivy's mom, with Mr. Wexler chiming in in the background.

Frankie nosed at the black stripe in Ivy's hair and let the comforting tones of Mrs. Wexler wash over them.

"Just wanted to call and give you an update," Mrs. Wexler continued. "Moving is annoying as ever, we had to buy even *more* boxes. Let us know if your suitcases arrive—I can't believe we paid all that extra money and they got *lost*! Ridiculous. It was lovely of KJ's roommates to give you their hand-me-downs, but you know how I feel about hand-me-downs. Besides, you barely know those girls. Anyhow! We miss you. Send us more photos when you can, alright? You look so beautiful and happy. Ivy, I still think you should straighten your hair."

Ivy snorted. "At least she didn't tell me to cut the black stripe out."

"You should tell her you're dying all of it bright green," Frankie whispered.

Ivy laughed, sliding her cool bare knees against Frankie's. Frankie dragged a finger up her spine, counting notches in the dim morning light. They only had one widow in this apartment, but since the apartment was basically one big room plus a bathroom, it did an okay job. It lit the place and it kept the plants alive: a lavender plant and a pot of chives shoved into the sunniest corner of the windowsill.

"Anyhow," Mrs. Wexler continued. "We've been watching this new talk show that seems so popular. Have you heard of Ellen DeGeneres? She seems like a nice lady. Sensible. Funny, but not *annoying* funny like so many celebrities. Well, we should let you go. Call soon! Love you!"

The answering machine beeped.

Frankie snapped Ivy's red ribbon against her neck. "Sweetheart."

"Ow. What?"

"Do you know who Ellen DeGeneres is?"

Ivy blinked the muzzy blink of someone who was still half in a dream.

"You know who she is. I'll remind you later." Frankie smiled into Ivy's hair, all nerves and hope. Maybe the Wexlers were finally getting a clue.

Ivy settled back into her with a sigh. "Nightmares?"

"Not many. You?"

"None," Ivy said. It wasn't quite a lie—Frankie had woken up around midnight to hear Ivy whimpering something about *dark* and *no* and *hungry*, but Ivy never remembered those when she woke up, just the hazy memory

91

of fear. And if Frankie soothed her back to sleep, she wouldn't even remember that.

Frankie didn't see the point of reminding her of those things waiting in the dark. She nodded. "When do we have to get up?"

Ivy twisted in her arms and stiffened. "Shit. Ten minutes ago."

"*Shit.*" Frankie sprang out of bed, almost clocking Ivy with her elbow. "Sorry."

"It's fine, *move!*"

Frankie bent to pick up the closest pair of jeans. Ivy had a chest of drawers on her side of the room, but Frankie's side was more of a floordrobe.

Ivy rooted around on her nightstand. "Where's—"

Frankie threw her the dry shampoo.

"Thanks." The air filled with the scent of peaches.

Frankie pulled a shirt on and checked the answering machine. Two messages were waiting: the one they'd just heard from Mrs. Wexler, and the voicemail from Milly Hart they'd gotten a few sentences through—*Hi, is this Ivy and Frankie? Lissiter passed your number along, you were wanting to talk to Kate Higgins*—before they stopped the message to make it to the bus on time. They would listen to it eventually. They just…didn't need the Bulldeen reminder. Not yet.

Halfway out the door, Ivy stopped. "Wait, do I have pottery after work? I promised Jen I'd give her book back. No, wait, it's Thursday."

Her hair was ruffled. Her shirt was stained with the pasta sauce they'd made last night, her cheek still imprinted with pillow creases. And she was here, standing in the doorway of her and Frankie's apartment.

Frankie's heart twisted in her chest. The trouble had left its marks on them: Ivy's bite marks; a scab she'd picked into her face had scarred over, leaving a permanent pockmark above her upper lip. Frankie's stab wound was still pink, they had twin scars from Ms. Marvin taking their blood, and Ivy still hadn't lost that gaunt look she'd picked up in the last few weeks in Bulldeen. There were still nightmares about April, about rot, about creatures lurking in the dark. Maybe, someday, those things would stalk out of the dark.

But not right now. Now they were safe, no one crossing the street to avoid them or spitting as they passed or staring at them in the supermarket. Well, some people stared. But *less*. No one looked at them with the deep, primal fear of Bulldeen locals trying to ignore the evil that nestled right under their noses.

Ivy blinked. "What? Something on my face?"

"One second." Frankie rummaged in her handbag.

"What's—" Ivy fell silent as Frankie held up a familiar tube of black lipstick. She gasped. "*Graveyard Dark!* You found it!"

"*KJ* found it. This little chemist downtown. Stay still."

Ivy stopped her victory dance and offered her chin. Frankie held it with gentle fingers, spreading the black lipstick on. From the gleam in Ivy's eyes, she was also thinking of the first time they'd done this: Frankie's room, all those years ago.

Frankie leaned back. "There. Perfect."

Ivy smacked her lips. "Aren't you going to do yours?"

Frankie kissed her, firm and long. She pulled back with a smile.

Ivy tidied up the edges with her fingers. "There," she said softly. "Perfect."

She took Frankie's hand. Frankie squeezed back, and they walked out into their new lives together.

END.

honeybloods

If you want to see how Frankie and Ivy are doing 15 years after their series ends, they make a cameo in HONEYBLOODS, my new sapphic vampire romance series.

HONEYBLOODS is a bite-sized sapphic vampire romance full of sweetness, snark, gore, and only one motel bed.

You can get HONEYBLOODS here.

thank you

Thank you so much for reading SWEETHEARTS!

If you want to support me, please leave a review on Goodreads, Amazon or any social media of your choice.

You can find out about my LGBT YA books and other exciting updates by subscribing to my newsletter! Sign up by visiting my website at isbelleauthor.com.

acknowledgments

First off, thank you to Elizabeth Kalbacher, who beta read every book in the BABYLOVE series. Thank you also to Catriona Turner and Edward Giordano for your editing work! And thank you to Laya Rose for the incredible cover art. You've all been a crucial part in helping Frankie and Ivy's story come to life, and I am so grateful.

about the author

I. S. Belle is a Young Adult author who lives in New Zealand. She has a Creative Writing Masters from the International Institute of Modern Letters. She works in a bookstore and stops to pat dogs in the street. If you have a dog and your local bookshop allows pets - for the love of booksellers, please bring them in.

You can find her on Tiktok @i.s.belle_writes and on Instagram @isbelleauthor.

also by i. s. belle

BABYLOVE SERIES

BABYLOVE
SUGARSNAP
SWEETHEARTS - Coming Soon

ZOMBABE

ZOMBABE

HONEYBLOODS SERIES

HONEYBLOODS - Coming 2024

GIRLS NIGHT

GIRLS NIGHT - Coming April 2024

Printed in Great Britain
by Amazon

38377585R00061